SCENE ONE,
TAKE TWO

"*Saved by the Bell*" titles include:

Mark-Paul Gosselaar: Ultimate Gold
Mario Lopez: High-Voltage Star
Behind the Scenes at "Saved by the Bell"
Beauty and Fitness with "Saved by the Bell"
Dustin Diamond: Teen Star
The "Saved by the Bell" Date Book

Hot new fiction titles:

SCENE ONE, TAKE TWO

by Beth Cruise

ALADDIN PAPERBACKS

Aladdin Paperbacks
An imprint of Simon & Schuster
Children's Publishing Division
1230 Avenue of the Americas
New York, NY 10020
First Aladdin Paperbacks edition 1995
Manufactured in the United States of America
10 9 8 7 6 5 4 3 2 1
Library of Congress Cataloging-in-Publication Data
Cruise, Beth.
Scene one, take two / by Beth Cruise. — 1st Aladdin Paperbacks ed.
p.   cm.
"Saved by the bell"—
Summary: When a local television station sponsors a contest with a
scholarship award to whoever makes the best promotional video for
Palisades, several of the "Saved by the Bell" gang decide to enter.
ISBN 0-689-80091-6
[1. Video recordings—Production and direction—Fiction. 2. Schools—
Fiction. 3. Friendship—Fiction.] I. Title.
PZ7.C88827Sc 1995
[Fic]—dc20   94-38344

**To
everyone
who's ever tried
to make their dreams
come true**

Chapter 1

▲ ▼ ▲ ▼ ▲

Zack Morris felt a heavy hand fall on his shoulder. He hastily swung the door of his locker closed and spun around.

"Morris." The familiar voice of Mr. Belding seemed to ring loudly in the hall despite the noise of students hurrying to their next class.

Zack plastered on his widest, most sincere smile. "Mr. Belding! Long time no see! How was your weekend? Don't you just love Monday morning? It's so great to be back at this fine institution. Hey, but you are looking great. I'll bet you've been jogging. Lost a few pounds, even."

"Forget it, Zack," Mr. Belding said. "I know a snow job when I hear one." He leaned forward and flicked Zack's locker open again. A two-foot wide piece of poster board fell out. "What's this?"

"That?" Zack tried to push the sheet back out of sight behind his dirty gym clothes. "Ah, it's my art project, sir. Ms. McCracken is teaching us about . . . er . . . pop art. You know, where a painting of a large soup can is worth megabucks. I'm really interested in it."

Mr. Belding plucked the poster out and studied it. "So I can see," he mused. "In fact, if I didn't know this was a project for your class, Zack, I'd swear that it looks just like the betting grid for a football pool."

Zack grabbed it away from him and pretended to study the neatly crossed lines. "You think? Wow, talk about realism!"

"It's a good thing it isn't a football pool, though," Mr. Belding said, "because, as you know, betting is against school rules, and if you were running a pool over the final outcome of Friday night's game, well, I'd be forced to suspend you."

"Whoa! Then it sure is a good thing this isn't what it looks like," Zack said, and shoved the poster back into his locker.

"Yes, it is," Mr. Belding agreed, a small smile curving his mouth. "Of course if it was, I would expect you to give back any money you had taken in."

"Absolutely. If it was a pool, you can bet . . . er, I mean you can rest assured that I would do exactly that," Zack answered.

Mr. Belding's smile grew wider. "Good, good," he said. "All the same, Morris, I think you and I will be seeing each other in detention this afternoon."

Zack sighed in resignation. "Yes, sir."

"Great." Mr. Belding turned away, paused, then turned back. "Do you really think I look like I lost weight?" he asked.

In a desperate attempt to butter the principal up, Zack nodded. "Positively, sir. Ten pounds, at least."

"Ten pounds," Mr. Belding echoed as if pleased with the sound of the words. "Perhaps I'll celebrate at lunch with a double tofuburger," he said as he went down the hall toward his office.

Zack smacked his head into the locker three quick times. Well, there went his extra money for this week. Not to mention the time after school that he'd planned to hang around the food court at the mall flirting with Kelly Kapowski, the sweetest, most beautiful girl ever to dish up dessert at Yogurt 4-U. He was just dying to find a way to inch back into her heart.

And a way to fill his rather empty wallet.

Maybe he should get a job.

The idea sent a shiver down Zack's spine, the same kind he got when report cards came out. Talk about scary!

Ever since his dad had decided to put the Morris family on the same one-payday-a-month plan he used at Intelpro, his small software company, Zack had some major money problems. His allowance looked like megafunds on the first, but he was bankrupt not long after that.

The gang wasn't very sympathetic when he had bemoaned his financial fate. Jessie Spano, his best friend and next-door neighbor since forever, told him to budget his cash.

The idea gave Zack double chills. It sounded like one of Mrs. Wozinski's home economics assignments, plan a household budget.

Well, fortunately, there were scads of other ways to make money, and he had all that time in detention to think about them. Situation flat busted wouldn't last for long.

Right now it was time to head for class or run into more problems with the school's own secret police, the hall monitors. And at this period he knew the head drill sergeant, Esther Colombine, was on duty. Next to Esther, vicious pit bulls were nothing but playful puppies.

Hearing the heavy thud of Esther's footsteps drawing near, Zack put his letter in track to good use and sped around a corner.

He nearly collided with A. C. Slater.

"Run," Zack gasped. "The Hound of the Bayside Halls is on the prowl."

Slater's grin carved deep dimples in his cheeks. "Not a problem, preppie," he said, and waved his signed hall pass in Zack's face. "At least, it isn't for some of us."

"Well, then, cut her off at the pass for me," Zack called, running a few steps backward. "See you later."

It was only when he was settled in his seat in history and the soothing sounds of Mrs. Wentworth's voice were nearly putting him to sleep that Zack began to wonder why Slater was roaming the halls.

This was the one period in the school day when Slater never missed his scheduled class. That was because it was a subject that interested Zack's muscle-bound friend—broadcasting. Slater was captain of both the football and wrestling teams now, but he was interested in becoming a sportscaster in the future. He even turned down a college scholarship at Great Bear University when he'd learned they were more interested in having a winning football team than they were in preparing their students for future careers.

Zack didn't know whether to be proud of his friend for turning down the scholarship, or if he should haul Slater off to have his head examined.

That didn't solve the mystery of what Slater was doing out of class, though.

"Mr. Morris, perhaps you can answer this question for us," Mrs. Wentworth said, interrupting Zack's musings.

Startled back to reality, Zack tried to look cool and collected. "Sure. No problema. What's the question?"

"Can you tell the class when the War of 1812 was fought?"

Aaahhhh. It sounded like a trick question. At

least Mrs. Wentworth didn't ask something really tough, like who'd *fought* the War of 1812.

He glanced at the clock on the wall. If only the bell would ring. The hands showed that the class was only half over.

He looked around at his fellow students, hoping to find a friend ready to mouth the answer at him. No one helped. He was stuck, cornered.

Zack took a deep breath. "The War of 1812 was fought in 1812," he said.

The class snickered. Even Mrs. Wentworth allowed a small grin to curve her lips.

"I'm afraid not entirely, Mr. Morris," Mrs. Wentworth murmured, and went on with her lecture without telling him where he'd gone wrong.

Zack slid lower in his seat. It looked as if nothing was going to go right for him that day.

▲   ▼   ▲

By the time lunch period arrived, Zack knew he was enduring the worst day of his life. Not only had he lost a really profitable scam, but he'd emptied his pockets paying back all the suckers he'd lined up. In gym class he had been trampled by a bunch of gorillas in a game of tag football. The gorillas never did get it through their heads that tag meant you *didn't* tackle your opponent, and he'd ended up beneath them a number of times.

Then, to top the day off, he'd seen Kelly smiling happily up into the face of Binky Grayson. Binky was a nice guy even if he had little charm and fewer looks. But he also had scads of money. As Zack eavesdropped, Binky explained in his lockjawed accent the difference between various brands of caviar to Kelly. She'd looked really interested, which was bad news for the dreams of Zack Morris.

If he didn't know Kelly so well, Zack would have thought she was paying attention to Binky because he was rich. But Kelly cared about people first, then friendship, world peace, becoming an actress, good grades, days at the beach, the latest Andy Prime song, the newest Mitch Tobias movie, if she looked good in the color purple, and then, *maybe,* she cared about money.

If Kelly dated Binky, though, he'd be able to take her to really nice places. How could Zack compete with stuff like that when there were moths building condominiums in his wallet?

Besides, Kelly had lots of reasons not to give him another chance. There were the girls, Dolores and Star and Alex and Tawnee Jo and Brandi and every other beauty he had ever laid his eyes on, and there were the scams.

He had to show Kelly that he'd changed, that he cared only about her, that he wasn't even interested in other girls.

Now there was a hard one. Especially with all the great-looking girls at Bayside.

But if getting Kelly back meant ignoring them—

all of them—even if they wore miniskirts and had gorgeous legs—well, he'd do it.

Give up scams, though? Whew! There was an even tougher one!

Unfortunately, since Mr. Belding had put a stop to Zack's immediate plan to get back into Kelly's heart, there was nothing more he could do for now but dream.

What he needed really badly, Zack decided as he came to the gang's usual table in the cafeteria, was to see Kelly smiling happily up at him. That would ease at least one of his worries.

A moment later she swung through the door.

She wasn't smiling, though. She was frowning.

The way his luck was running, it was a good thing Mr. Belding had nixed the football pool. Some sore loser would probably have blackened his eye.

"Hi, Zack," Kelly greeted, her usually smooth brow creased by lines of worry. "Have you seen Slater lately? He's acting really weird."

Zack's spirits sank even lower. She was worried about Slater. Not good. It wasn't long ago that Kelly and Slater had been dating. It hadn't worked out, thank goodness, but all the same, it had driven Zack nuts.

"Weird in what way exactly?" he asked carefully.

Kelly gave him a disgusted look and sat down. "There aren't varying degrees of weird in this case. We're talking about Slater, not Screech," she said.

Samuel "Screech" Powers skidded to a stop by the table just as she said that. "Oh, good," he said with a goofy grin. "I'm glad you weren't talking about me. I would have been worried if you'd been talking about me and my ears weren't burning."

"I'm worried about Slater," Kelly explained.

Screech's mobile face went all dopey-looking. "Ah, that's so sweet, Kelly. Does that mean you got back together with him?"

Zack gave his friend a smack on the shoulder to discourage that line of thought. Screech staggered.

"She just thinks Slater's acting weird," Zack explained.

"Wow!" Screech looked impressed. "How can you tell?"

"Hi!" Jessie Spano dropped her books on the table and took a seat next to Kelly. "What's up?"

"We were just talking about—"

Lisa Turtle dashed up breathlessly and nearly fell into the chair across from Kelly. "Slater just ignored me in the hall," she announced without bothering to greet everyone. "He is acting really weird."

"Boy, is he," Kelly said. "Have you noticed anything different about him lately, Jessie?"

Zack hurriedly sat in the only chair left near Kelly while Screech took the one next to Lisa. She scooted her chair away from his so that they wouldn't rub shoulders.

"So what was Slater doing?" Zack asked.

"Well," Kelly began, "he's avoiding all of us, for one thing. He wasn't at the Max after school last Friday."

"Neither was Zack," Screech pointed out.

Zack glared at him from across the table. Could he help it if the detention room was beginning to be a second home to him?

"I was spending quality time with Mr. Belding," Zack explained. "But speaking of acting weird, I ran into Slater in the hall this morning and—get this—he had a hall pass!"

"That's nothing," Kelly said. "When I passed the football field earlier, he was standing in the middle of it, staring at the goalposts."

"Maybe he was planning his strategy for the game this week," Zack suggested.

"I don't think so," Kelly declared, the worried look coming back into her pretty eyes. "He was holding his hands up, creating a squared-off area to peer through."

"That's pretty weird," Jessie agreed.

"I'll say," Lisa added.

Screech heaved a giant sigh of relief. "Slater was probably just blocking for shooting," he told them. "That's what directors do in the movie biz, you know."

"Oh, of course," Kelly said, her bright smile returning. "He's probably working on a project for his broadcasting class. They do learn something about filmmaking in it."

"I don't think so," Zack muttered. "When I saw Slater in the hall, it was *during* his broadcasting class."

Chapter 2

▲ ▼ ▲ ▼ ▲

Kelly's smile disappeared. Well, that was all right, Zack thought, because he didn't want her smiling when she was thinking about Slater. Still, their friend's strange behavior did merit checking out.

Zack dropped an arm around Kelly's shoulders. "Don't worry. I'll find out what Slater's up to."

"Me, too," Screech insisted. "After all, if Zack Bond is on the case again, then Arnold Benedict will be at his side. We're a secret agent team."

Zack nearly groaned out loud. The last time he and Screech had spied on someone it was the head cheerleader from Bayside's arch rival, Valley High. Their covert operation hadn't gone according to plan. In fact, it had totally backfired!

Still, he couldn't be everywhere, Zack admitted. And if he could send Screech out shadowing Slater, that would leave him with more time to spend with Kelly.

"Okay," Zack said, and motioned his friends to lean closer. "Here's the plan. First, we . . ."

▲ ▼ ▲

When the final bell of the day rang and Zack dragged toward detention, he was sure his disastrous day was behind him. Nothing more could happen to him in detention, Zack figured as he nodded to Mr. Belding in the front of the room and took a seat in front of Butch Maxwell, another detention regular. Zack slouched down low and breathed a sigh of relief. He was safe.

Or so he thought until a pretty redhead with really pale skin and a short skirt strolled into the room, tripped over Butch's outstretched legs, and dumped a ton of books on Zack's head.

"Oops," she said, regaining her balance.

"Zack!" Mr. Belding cried, jumping up from his desk. "Are you all right, son?"

Zack rubbed his head and wondered if the avalanche had disturbed the perfection of his blond hair. Never mind if his brains were rattling around. They'd been that way since the football pileup in gym class. Of course, he could always play up the accident and get out of detention.

The girl stepped over the books on the floor, dropped down in the seat next to him, plopped her chin in her hand, and stared at him with the largest blue eyes Zack had ever seen.

"Sorry, luv," she said in a lightly accented voice. "Should we call the casualty ward and have a nurse give you a look round?"

"Emergency room," Mr. Belding murmured, sounding a bit distracted. "Good idea, Clorinda. I'll call 911."

"How's the old noodle feeling, dearie?" Clorinda asked.

Zack carefully checked his head. Nothing seemed to be broken, and there didn't seem to be a hair out of place. "I'll live," he said.

"You're sure?" Mr. Belding asked. He looked ready to sprint off in search of paramedics. He waved a hand in front of Zack's eyes. "How many fingers am I holding up?"

"Three."

Mr. Belding looked worried. "Three?" He looked at his hand. "Oh, so I am. Can I get you anything, Zack? Ice pack, water, aspirin?"

"Shorter detention?" Zack asked hopefully.

Mr. Belding grinned with relief. "Now I know you're okay," he said. "But the answer is, not a chance."

After Mr. Belding had resettled at his desk, the redheaded girl laughed softly. "So, what are you in for, luv?" she whispered. "Me, I'm a victim of the jolly bailiff in the hall."

Even if she'd given him a concussion, Zack was in total sympathy with the girl. Anybody who'd had a run in with Esther Colombine deserved it. "I'm a victim of the free enterprise system," he said, and held out his hand. "Zack Morris."

She slipped a soft hand in his. "Clorinda Winter of Great Britain . . . that's England to you Yanks."

"First day here?" Zack asked.

Clorinda nodded. "Lovely way to welcome visitors to your foreign shores, isn't it? Jailing them straight away."

Zack grinned at her. "Happen to you often?"

She laughed again. It was a light tinkling sound. "All the time."

"Then it looks like we'll be seeing a lot of each other. And always in this room," he said.

Clorinda's lashes dipped flirtatiously. "Oh, must it always be here? Don't you American chaps walk out with girls outside of school?"

"You mean date? Oh, well, sure we do." Zack felt a stab of conscience. Clorinda was cute and all that, but if he was going to convince Kelly that she was the only girl for him, redheaded foreign students were definitely off-limits. He was never going to let another girl come between him and Kelly Kapowski ever again. And to prove it to Kelly, he would stay far away from Clorinda Winter.

"It's just that . . . ," Zack mumbled, searching for the right words.

Clorinda sighed and leaned back. "That's okay, dearie. I understand. A handsome chappie like you probably already has a girl. We can just be friends."

She brushed back an unruly red curl and gave Zack a slow smile. "If things don't work out with her, just remember I'll be waiting, luv. Help me pick my books up?"

Zack breathed a sigh of relief. He'd made it through the first test. If only Kelly knew.

Then Clorinda bent over to pick up one of her books and gave him an impish grin. "If your head hurts, Zack, I could always kiss it to make it better," she offered.

Her hair was gorgeous, her eyes were even more so, and her legs . . .

Zack swallowed loudly. It looked as if the test wasn't quite over yet. And worse yet, there was a good chance he was going to flunk it big-time!

▲   ▼   ▲

Having successfully avoided tangles with Mr. Belding and Esther Colombine, Zack skipped being stuck in detention the next day. Instead, he met the gang at the Max after school. Slater, however, was missing.

Everyone else was there, though: Jessie and Lisa and Screech and Kelly. Screech was sitting next to Kelly in the booth. Zack took care of that situation by pulling Screech to his feet and sliding into the booth next to Kelly. "Anything to report?" he asked everyone.

Screech fell back into a nearby chair.

"Not much," Jessie said. "I made sure I took a seat next to Slater in physics class. And, boy, was he ever acting strange!"

The gang leaned forward eagerly.

"The muscle-bound Neanderthal was actually taking notes on the subject matter," Jessie said, clearly stunned at the revelation herself. "Can you believe it?"

The gang recoiled in horror.

"Eww." Lisa gave a shiver. "That's creepy."

"I'll say," Zack agreed.

"But it's nothing compared to what happened when I cornered Slater sixth period," Lisa continued.

They all leaned forward again.

"Well," Lisa confided, "you know how great Slater always looks?"

"Yeah," Kelly and Jessie agreed in unison, their voices a bit dreamy.

Zack frowned.

"The hunk asked me for advice on wardrobe planning," Lisa said.

Zack turned to Screech. "Now that is really scary," he said. He and Screech both gave exaggerated shivers.

Lisa glared at them. "Some people care about how they look," she insisted.

Screech's curly hair bounced as he agreed. "That's true. I spend hours each evening planning what to wear the next day. It takes a lot of hard work to come up with outfits like this," he proclaimed proudly, hooking his thumbs behind his chartreuse suspenders.

Ms. McCracken, the art teacher, had been heard to say Screech used an amazing amount of imagination in his color choices, but Mr. Monza, the head of Bayside's maintenance department, had said he couldn't look at Screech's wardrobe without getting dizzy.

"Slater said he wanted a new look, something more authoritative," Lisa revealed.

"Authoritative?" Jessie repeated. "Maybe this isn't really Slater we're dealing with. It sounds more like his doppelganger."

Screech's mouth dropped open. "Wow!" he breathed in awe. "An alien being! I wonder if he's got antennas hidden in his hair that he uses to contact his friends in the spacecraft?"

Jessie tossed one of her french fries at him. Screech caught it in his mouth and beamed at her as he chewed.

"A doppelganger isn't from outer space, dork," she said. "It is a person's double."

Screech nodded sagely. "That makes sense. If I was Slater and had a bunch of football goons galloping down the field at me, I'd want a stunt double, too."

Kelly's eyes were wide. "You mean Slater might not be Slater?"

"It's one explanation for his strange behavior," Jessie said. "What did you learn, Kelly?"

Kelly sighed sadly. "Nothing," she moaned. "Zack and I drove to every junk food restaurant within a mile of the school at lunch, looking for Slater, but we never found him."

"How could you?" Lisa asked. "He was right in the cafeteria."

Kelly turned accusing eyes on Zack.

"Hey, I heard he was bypassing the broccoli surprise Ms. Meadows was serving today," he insisted.

"The only person who goes out of their way to avoid broccoli is you, Zack," Kelly reminded him, and turned to Jessie, her expression worried once more. "Do you really think someone has kidnapped Slater and put a look-alike in his place?"

"No," Jessie said. "But I do think Slater is acting very un-Slater-like. I wish we knew why."

"Guess we'll have to corner him and ask," Zack said.

"Great!" Screech added. "Because I want to find out if he knows about this." He fished in the pocket of his green-and-blue checked pants and pulled out a piece of paper. It was folded as neatly as a road map.

"What is it?" Lisa asked.

Zack whisked it away from Screech, opened it, and quickly read the large-sized print.

Win College Scholarship Money!!!!!
KPSD, Television Channel 17,
and the Palisades Visitors Bureau
want you to produce a video!
Just film a five-minute segment
showing what a great place
Palisades is to visit.

> **The contest is open to any
> graduating senior in a
> Palisades high school.
> First prize is a
> $1,000 college scholarship.
> Winner to be announced at the
> Surf's Up Beach Party.**

Zack let the sheet of paper float to the table. "I think," he announced, "we've finally found out exactly what Slater is up to."

Chapter 3
▲ ▼ ▲ ▼ ▲

Screech smacked his forehead. "Of course! Why didn't I think of that?"

"Well, if Slater really is working on a video for this contest, he needs help," Jessie said.

"What do you mean?" Lisa demanded. "It's a great idea!"

"No, I mean, Slater really needs help. *Our* help so he can win. We all know how important college scholarship money is," Jessie explained. "But to win it will take a lot of imagination and forethought. Slater's experience lies in areas where muscle power outranks brainpower."

"Oh, I don't know," Zack murmured. "I've seen him do some pretty imaginative handling of a football. Like in the final play before halftime last week."

Screech's eyes widened in surprise. "That was imaginative? I thought it was a fumble!"

The girls ignored them.

"Winning the contest would look really great on his college applications," Kelly added.

"And with me as his fashion consultant," Lisa said, "Slater will not only look good when he gives his acceptance speech, he'll look GOOO-OOOD."

"Okay. Then let's do it!" Jessie urged.

"Do what?" Zack asked.

"I think she means we should help Slater," Screech said.

"I know what she means. I mean, *how* are we going to help Slater?"

Screech thought a moment. "I could hold the camera for him. Or maybe write a musical sound track and play it on my kazoo."

"That ought to clinch it for him," Zack muttered under his breath.

"I'll do wardrobe and makeup," Lisa offered.

"It isn't much," Kelly said, "but I have been in a commercial and auditioned for a television show. I could give Slater the benefit of my experience."

"Then I'll handle creative input," Jessie declared. "The object is to show what a great place Palisades is to visit, right? If left on his own, I'll bet Slater would show five minutes of girls in bikinis on the beach."

Zack nudged Screech. "Sounds good to me,"

he said. "I never see enough of girls in bikinis."

Jessie frowned at him. "I don't know why anthropologists are digging in cave sites for examples of primitive man. They could just study specimens like you and Slater right here at Bayside High."

"Hey! Don't link me with the missing link," Zack insisted.

Kelly giggled. "You know Jessie doesn't mean it when she calls you a Neanderthal, Zack."

"Who says I don't?" Jessie demanded.

"Well, seeing a bunch of great-looking guys would sure get me to visit Palisades if I didn't already live here," Lisa said. "Maybe I should volunteer to be one of the girls on the beach. I could even squeeze one of the guys' biceps and look thrilled. Heck, I *would* be thrilled!"

Jessie frowned at her in condemnation.

"Well, I would be," Lisa defended. "Can I help it if it's fun? I've got this really cute new bikini, too."

"I wouldn't rush into this," Zack warned. "We don't know for sure that Slater is doing a video for this contest. We're just guessing."

"True," Screech said, a thoughtful look on his face. "We could ask him, though."

"Oh, sure. Just like that, huh?" Zack said. "Get real. What do you propose we do? Walk up to him and say, 'Slater, have you entered the Channel 17 scholarship contest?'"

A heavy hand fell on Zack's shoulder. Zack

cringed, almost expecting to see Mr. Belding standing behind him again.

"Yes, preppie, I am entering the video contest," Slater said. "How did you guess?"

"Oh, just little things," Zack said as Slater spun a chair around and straddled it. "Like possession of a hall pass."

"Hey! Mr. Elkins sent me to Belding's office to get a new attendance record for him," Slater explained. "The contest is a great idea, isn't it? I think I can win this one, too."

"We want you to," Jessie assured him. "And that's why we are all going to help you."

"Help me?" Slater looked at her blankly. "No offense, momma, but I kind of think I should do this on my own."

"Of course you do, Slater," Kelly soothed. "But what with the football season in full swing . . ."

"And all those little time-consuming details to see to," Lisa added.

"And a script to work out," Jessie reminded.

". . . well, we want to pitch in and do what we can to make things easier for you," Kelly ended.

Slater gave them his slow grin. "Thanks, guys. It isn't that I don't appreciate the offer, but I really want to do everything on this myself."

The girls exchanged worried looks.

"Wait a minute," Slater said, suspicious now of their intentions. "You weren't thinking you'd like a cut of the money for yourselves, were you?"

"Of course not," Jessie assured him.

"Not a chance, sugar," Lisa declared.

"How can you say that, Slater?" Kelly demanded, her voice sounding hurt.

"Besides, couldn't we just enter the contest ourselves?" Screech asked.

"No reason why you couldn't," Slater said.

"Sure, why not?" Zack asked. "Money is going to be tight for college for all of us."

"I'll say," Kelly murmured. "But making a video is more in line with what you want to do when you get out of school, Slater. Winning this contest would mean more to you than just scholarship money."

Jessie nodded. "Absolutely. And that's why you shouldn't turn down any help you can get. Look what networking did to help us stop the destruction of the desert."

By contacting an old friend of her mother's to bring a local environmental issue to the attention of a television reporter, Jessie had experienced the benefits of networking firsthand.

"Yeah, sure," Slater mumbled, still suspicious. "Do you also swear that your sudden interest in this isn't to check out what I'm working on so you can steal it and win the contest yourself?"

Jessie's mouth dropped open in shock. "How can you think I would do such a thing?"

Slater shrugged. "I've seen you do some really

weird things, momma. It pays to never underestimate the competition."

"That's true," Screech said with feeling. "When I let Belinda Towser see the plans for my hamster habitat, little did I know she was engaged in industrial espionage. By upscaling my idea to an apartment complex complete with swimming pool, she neatly whisked first place in the science competition away from me."

"A truly sad day in the world of science," Zack agreed, shaking his head sadly. "It makes a person wonder about their so-called friends."

"It does indeed," Slater said, still watching Jessie for signs that she was planning a Belinda Towser trick herself.

"Men!" Jessie growled in frustration. "What do I have to do to prove that I'm trustworthy?"

Slater gave the matter some thought and consumed the rest of Jessie's french fries as he did so. "I suppose you could sign an official statement to the effect that you do not think, will not think, and have never thought about entering Channel 17's contest," he suggested.

Kelly nodded. "That would work. We could all do one and witness each other's signatures."

Lisa held up her hands in protest. "Hey, all I'm offering is wardrobe consultation. A thousand dollars wouldn't even put a dent in my shopping budget for college. Besides, I don't even know how to operate my parents' video camera."

"Well, if that's what it takes to prove myself to you, Slater, then I'll sign a document," Jessie offered, and flipping open her notebook, ripped a sheet of paper from it. "Just tell me what to write."

"Uh . . ."

Zack placed a restraining hand on Slater's arm. "Let me handle this to make sure all the loopholes are covered."

"Loopholes!" Jessie fumed.

Slater considered. "And just what is it going to cost me, preppie?"

"Cost? Would I charge a friend for something like this? I'm merely performing a valuable service because I need to see justice done. In fact—"

"Like I said," Slater repeated, "what's it going to cost me?"

Zack grinned. He happened to know that Slater had recently made a very comfortable bit of money by doing oil changes on some of the cheerleaders' cars and those of their parents. "Well, a couple of Max-imum burgers would not go amiss."

"Broke again, huh?" Slater said with a knowing grin.

While Slater placed the order, Zack leaned back in the booth and stretched, one hand behind his head, the other resting along the back of the seat, a millimeter or so from Kelly's shoulders. All she had to do was lean back and things would begin to look right in his world.

Kelly leaned forward instead. "You don't have to do this, Jessie."

"But you thought it was a good idea," Jessie said.

"Only on a volunteer basis."

"And this is definitely not that," Lisa added.

"No. If this is the only way Slater will trust me, then I'm doing it," Jessie declared. She gave her long curly hair a defiant toss over her shoulders. "Tell me what to write, Zack."

"Let's make it short and to the point," he suggested. "Something like, *I, Jessica Amelia Spano, being of sound mind . . .*"

Jessie ground her teeth.

"Did you say something?"

"I, Jessica Amelia Spano, being of sound mind," Jessie parroted as she wrote.

"Do solemnly swear that I have no ulterior motives in offering to assist Albert Clifford Slater . . ."

Jessie's pen faltered a bit. She did have an ulterior motive, she admitted to herself. It wasn't to make a video, though. She just wanted Slater back as her steady boyfriend. Perhaps if they spent a lot of time working on his video, he'd remember all the fun they once had together. At least they'd had fun when they weren't fighting. But that was all Slater seemed to remember.

Biting her lip to keep from commenting on Zack's wording, Jessie continued to write.

". . . and that if I so much as pick up a camera to

film my own video after giving such assistance, I will
forfeit the right to be trusted without prior proof in all
future dealings with Albert Clifford Slater."

"Geez, preppie. Do you have to say my full name
quite so loud?" Slater demanded. "There's a reason I
don't use it, you know."

"In all future dealings with Albert Clifford
Slater," Jessie repeated out loud.

Two cute blond girls at the next table looked up.
"Albert Clifford?" they said to each other.

"See," Slater hissed, slumping low in his seat.

Jessie signed the sheet of paper with a flourish
and passed it to both Lisa and Kelly to sign as wit-
nesses. "Here you are, Slater. Now do you trust me?"
she asked as she handed over the statement.

"It wasn't so much a matter of trusting you, Jess,"
Slater said, admiring her written promise a moment
before tucking it in his jeans pocket. "I just think
winning would mean a lot more to me if I did the
project myself."

"I can understand that," she assured him. "But
wouldn't it be handy to have an assistant to help you
with little details?"

"Tedious things like sharpening pencils and running out for burgers," Zack explained helpfully.

"Now, that I could get into," Slater agreed. "Are
those the kinds of things you had in mind, Jess?"

Jessie's teeth clamped together in a tight smile. It
wasn't exactly what she had in mind, but to spend

time with Slater she would do it. She hoped he would realize that they were a great team, both fun and productive, and he'd ask her to go out with him again.

"If that's what needs to be done, then I'll do it," she vowed.

Slater grinned widely, his dimples flashing. "Then, momma, you just got yourself a job."

Chapter 4

▲ ▼ ▲ ▼ ▲

An hour later, Jessie stretched out on a lawn chair, content for the moment just to enjoy the sight of Slater lounging in the hammock in her backyard once more.

The afternoon was gorgeous, the sky blue and dotted with fluffy little clouds, the air warm but cooled by a soft breeze off the Pacific Ocean. Dappled shadows shaded both her chair and the hammock that was strung between two large old trees. It was the kind of afternoon when even an overachiever like herself was tempted to kick back and enjoy life in Palisades.

Jessie sighed. Enough of this lazing about. It was time to get started on Slater's video. The deadline was five days away, which didn't leave much time to work on it, even if the finished product need only be five minutes long.

"So, Slater," she said. "What has to be done first? What are you planning on for the theme of your video?"

Slater didn't answer. The hammock rocked softly to and fro. Birds sang in the trees. Farther down the street, Jessie could hear the sound of children playing, and closer at hand, she could hear Zack's stereo blasting out the latest CD by Andy Prime, Kelly's favorite singer.

"Slater?" Jessie called.

A soft snore was all the answer she got.

"Slater!" Jessie shouted.

Still no answer.

Disgusted, Jessie got to her feet, grabbed hold of one side of the hammock, and tipped Slater out.

"Huh? What?" he mumbled, waking up when he hit the ground.

"Oh, I'm sorry. I must have overturned you when I tried to put a pillow beneath your head," Jessie said innocently.

"Pillow? What pillow?" Slater asked, still drowsy.

"That one," Jessie declared, and pointed to one six feet away on her lounge chair. "Since you're awake, though, maybe we should talk about your ideas for the contest."

Slater pushed to his feet. "The plan is to win," he said.

"I know that. How are you going to do it? What is your subject?"

Slater's dimples deepened. "The title says it all, momma. I'm calling it *Sports Are Great in Palisades*."

Jessie shook her head as if to clear it of cobwebs. "Excuse me? Isn't that kind of a boring title?"

"Boring?" Slater's dimples disappeared. "What do you mean? It's clear, concise, and it says exactly what I'm going to show in my video."

"It's still boring," Jessie said. "You need something clever, witty, catchy for a title. Something like, er, well, like *Sports Shorts from Palisades*."

"*Sports Shorts?*" Slater repeated in disbelief. "It sounds like a fashion show."

"It was just an example," Jessie hastened to explain. "I didn't mean you had to use it."

"That's for sure," Slater mumbled.

"So, what kind of sports are you going to feature?"

"Football, soccer, tennis, surfing . . ."

"I knew the beach would get in there somehow," Jessie said under her breath.

Slater heard her. "And just what does that mean?"

Jessie wished she'd kept her mouth shut. "Just that the beach is a . . . a fun and exciting part of life in Palisades," she declared, flashing him a quick smile. "I think it's a great idea."

"No, you don't. I know you better than that, Jess. You think it's stupid, trite, and predictable."

"I do not. Well, maybe a little. Sure, we've got some really great beaches here. But, Slater, there are so many great things you can show about Palisades that don't even involve the beach. We're just another beach community among a thousand or so along the West Coast. It would be more interesting to tourists to discover the other attractions, the things that make Palisades different from all those other places."

Slater scooped up the pillow from the lounge chair and flopped back into the hammock again. "This is my video, and I'm doing it my way."

Jessie choked back another argument. She was not going to convince Slater that she was a fun person to be with if she started a fight with him over a stupid thing like a video.

"That's fine, Slater. I admire you for sticking to your concept. Just tell me where we start and what you want me to do."

Slater stared up into the leafy bower overhead. He gave the hammock a little shove to set it swinging and put his hands behind his head. "Lemonade would be nice," he suggested. "Maybe some corn chips and salsa, too."

"You want food?"

"Just a snack," Slater said. "For now. You did promise, Jess."

Only in a moment of weakness, she thought. "Fine. I'll be right back. Try not to fall asleep again," Jessie snapped shortly, and let the screen door slam shut behind her.

Five minutes later she was back. "Your drink and

your munchies," Jessie said, setting a tray down on his chest. She didn't care if he spilled everything all over himself. It would serve him right for treating her like a servant. And for enjoying doing it.

Slater barely opened his eyes long enough to pick up the frosted glass. He took a sip and nearly bolted upright. "This isn't lemonade," he gasped, quickly catching the tray before it toppled. "And where are the corn chips? These are vegetables."

"We were out of lemonade, so I gave you lime juice in mineral water. And the carrot and celery sticks are better for you than corn chips and salsa. If you like, I can add broccoli, cauliflower, and some fresh mushrooms to your snack."

Slater winced. "Don't bother."

Jessie stretched out on the lounge chair again. "Okay, your topic is sports in Palisades. What are you going to film first?"

Slater chomped down on a celery stick. "I was thinking about heading out to the Half Moon Country Club and getting some tennis on film."

"That sounds good," Jessie told him, impressed that Slater actually had a plan in mind. "Some of the members are tournament-class players. Palisades could be billed as Wimbledon-on-the-Pacific and attract all kind of visitors to the courts here. Not just those at the Half Moon, but there are some nice ones at the better hotels where they would be staying. I could check with my dad since he's in the hotel business. You shouldn't forget the city park courts either. Maybe expand to include handball and . . ." Jessie paused in her list of suggestions, belatedly remembering that this was Slater's project, not hers. "That is, you could do those things if you wanted to," she hastened to assure him.

"I was thinking more about shooting footage of a couple of really cute girls knocking a ball around," Slater said. "Do you remember the three blonds who gave Kelly all that trouble when she was a waitress at the club house? What did she call them? The Triple A's?"

"Are you referring to Amber Porterhouse and her friends?" Jessie demanded, her voice cold enough to form icebergs.

Even the crew of the Titanic would have reversed engines and steamed away to safety at the sound. Slater plowed on ahead unaware of the danger.

"Yeah," he said. "Oh, hey, didn't Zack date Amber? Maybe he can use his influence to get her and her friends to wear their shortest tennis skirts and jump around a lot. That would make a great start for the video."

Jessie ground her teeth. "Considering that Zack helped Kelly prove Amber's brother was harassing her on the job, and got him fired, I don't think Amber would be too thrilled to talk to Zack, much less do any favors for him."

Slater frowned. "I forgot about that. Well, there are other great-looking girls at the Half Moon."

"There's also the tennis pro and the players training for the tournament circuit," Jessie reminded.

"Sure, but do they look as good as those girls in tiny little white skirts? I don't think so," Slater said.

Jessie counted to ten slowly. "Okay, then what comes after the tennis shots?"

Slater considered and bit into a carrot stick. "Football, maybe. We've got the game against Winkleford Vocational High on Friday."

"Football," Jessie repeated. "I suppose you are going to turn the camera on the cheerleaders and have them do their highest kicks."

"Not a bad idea," Slater admitted, "but I was going to concentrate on the players."

"Oh." Both the Winkleford and Bayside teams had players who had been drafted for an All-California squad during the preseason. Shots of local football heroes, some of whom were probably on their way to careers with professional teams, would be impressive. If national tennis greats were out, well, hometown football stars were an acceptable replacement.

"Wasn't Dennis Winkleford, founder of the vocational school, once a professional player in the big leagues?" Jessie asked. "If you added an interview with him and some of the players, found out if there will be any scouts from universities attending, and then showed these same players doing some community service like working with underprivileged kids . . ." Jessie stopped when she realized Slater had stopped chomping on his snack of vegetables.

"Actually," Slater said, "I was going to add a little beefcake to the cheesecake. There is nothing that gets girls excited like the sight of hunks in uniforms."

Pushed to her limit, Jessie got to her feet and strode purposefully toward the hammock. "How about showing that Palisades is a caring community? How about showing the great strides that have been made to fight air pollution and clean up the water in Palisades Creek? How about the fact that a lot of positions of authority in the local government are held by women and minorities? How about . . ."

"How about getting me a refill on that lime juice stuff?" Slater asked. "It was pretty good."

Jessie grabbed the hammock and dumped him out on the ground again. Carrot and celery sticks flew everywhere. "How about taking you and your stupid ideas out of my yard?" she stormed. "I can't believe you want to show Palisades as a place where guys do nothing but ogle girls and girls do nothing but ogle guys!"

"So I'll show them playing volleyball on the beach, too," Slater said. "But I think I'll save that as the closing bit."

"Out!" Jessie insisted. "To make sure Channel 17 has a decent entry in their contest, I guess I'll just have to enter it myself."

"You can't," Slater reminded her, getting to his feet. He pulled the statement she'd written and signed in front of everyone else out of his pocket. "This says that you can't."

Jessie ripped it out of his hand, tore it into small pieces, and threw it over Slater's head like confetti. "Now I can make my own video," she announced. "And I not only intend to do so, I intend to win the contest, too. Stuff that in your trough and eat it, bucko."

Slater scooped up the pieces of paper, then leaned back against one of the trees and folded his arms. He wasn't dumb enough to get back in the hammock again. "Looks like I was right not to trust you, Jess."

The words were like cold water thrown over her. Jessie got hold of her temper, aghast that she'd let it get out of hand. What was it about Slater that made her lose control? Hadn't she promised herself that she would not start a fight? That this time Slater would see her as a fun and helpful companion?

So much for good intentions.

"I'm sorry, Slater. You're right. I did promise. Tearing up that sheet of paper didn't change anything."

"Yes, it did, Jess," he said softly, and pushed away from the tree. "I'm just sorry it didn't work out for us. It never does, does it?"

"Slater."

"Forget it, Jess. Enter the contest. Make your own video. Show me up, why don't you? Prove that your way is right and my way is wrong. Win it, Jess. Win the stupid contest," Slater dared.

Jessie watched him walk out the gate, get in his truck, and drive off down the street. She'd blown it again. Blown her chance with Slater. This time there was no way he was ever going to forgive her. She wasn't sure she could forgive herself.

Unless . . .

Jessie flopped down in the hammock and stared up into the tree branches overhead. Unless, she mused, she did make her own video and win the contest. That would show Slater that she'd only been trying to help him. That if he had accepted even some of her suggestions, he could have walked off with the scholarship money.

Now, which concept was the most logical to follow?

When Mrs. Spano got home from work, Jessie was still swinging in the hammock and thinking.

Chapter 5

▲ ▼ ▲ ▼ ▲

Slater drove around the block, parked, and slunk back to Zack's house. To make sure Jessie was unaware of his return, Slater climbed up the tree outside Zack's bedroom and entered through the window.

Zack wasn't even aware that he had a visitor. He was sacked out in a beanbag chair, a gogglelike visor strapped over his eyes, his hands covered with gloves. Wires connected the gloves to the visor. Every once in a while he'd wiggle his fingers, move his head, and say "All right!" in a satisfied tone.

Slater shut the window and locked it, then turned the blaring stereo off. "Preppie," he called softly.

Zack chuckled and wiggled his fingers some more.

"Preppie," Slater said a bit louder. When he got no answer, he punched Zack in the arm to get his attention.

"Ow!" Zack cried. He moved to rub his shoulder and then dodged back in his seat. "Whoa! That was a close one!"

"Preppie?" Slater snapped. "What are you doing?"

Zack removed the visor and then the gloves. "Virtual reality," he explained. "Screech lent it to me. He invented a program that lets you explore Mars. I was scaling the side of one of the canals when these weird-looking creatures started swarming down the rock wall. Well, maybe they weren't all that weird-looking. One of them reminded me of Screech!"

Slater sat on the side of the bed and leaned forward, his forearms resting on his knees. "I need help, Zack."

"I've always known that," Zack said. "I just never expected you to admit it."

"I mean it," Slater insisted.

"Sure you do. Here, see what you think of Mars." Zack handed the visor over. "I'm thinking of talking my dad into expanding his computer software company to sell virtual reality stuff. The market's there. All it takes is a little push and—"

Slater shoved the visor back into Zack's hand. "I don't have time to play silly games."

"Silly games?" Zack stared at Slater as if he had suddenly grown antennas like the green men of virtual reality Mars. He had to remember to point out to his father that the program would do especially well at Christmas. The green inhabitants on the red planet had looked really cheerful.

"I need help on this video for the contest," Slater admitted. "I didn't originally, but now with Jessie as competition, I need all the help I can get."

Zack shook his head back and forth a couple of times fast. "Sorry. I guess my brain is still in virtual reality. I thought you said you needed help *and* that Jessie was entering Channel 17's contest."

"I did and she is."

"Can't be. For one thing, Jessie made a solemn vow she wouldn't film her own entry. I dictated it and she signed it."

Slater reached in his shirt pocket and gathered a handful of confetti. He let it drift down to the floor. "Does this tell you anything about that vow?"

"A little," Zack admitted. "What happened?"

"What didn't happen?" Slater groaned. "You know how Jessie is. She tried to take over. She didn't like anything I had planned."

"Mmm," Zack agreed. "That sounds like Jessie. What else happened?"

Slater grimaced. "She made me eat vegetables."

Zack shivered.

"And she claims she is going to win the contest. You've got to stop her, preppie. I can't have a girl beat me at this. Especially not Jessie."

"So what do you want me to do?" Zack asked.

"What else? I want you to spy on her, find out what she's doing, and make sure she fails."

"That's all?"

Slater considered a moment. "Well, you wouldn't happen to have some corn chips and salsa handy, would you? I've really got to get the taste of celery and carrots out of my mouth. It's nasty."

▲   ▼   ▲

Kelly stared at Jessie in disbelief. "You didn't!" she exclaimed.

"I did!" Jessie said with a groan. She dropped back full length on Kelly's bed. Once dinner was over, she'd told her mother she was studying with Kelly and rushed over to her friend's house.

"I could hear myself but I couldn't stop. So I've blown it with Slater for good. Unless I can show him that I was right in this case and that everything I said was to help him, not to cut him down."

Kelly wrinkled her nose. "I don't know if you can ever do that, Jessie. Guys hate it when girls prove they know best."

Jessie stared at the ceiling, preferring not to meet Kelly's eyes when she asked the question she was dying to know the answer to. "Did you have that kind of trouble when you were dating Slater?"

"Me?" Kelly giggled. "Jessie, guys don't usually talk about that kind of stuff to me. They're too busy trying to be romantic."

"Slater, romantic?"

"Yeah. In fact, Slater is the most romantic guy I've ever dated," Kelly said.

Jessie propped herself up on her elbows. "*Slater?*" she asked in disbelief. "*Our* A. C. Slater?"

"Yep," Kelly agreed.

"You're kidding," Jessie insisted. "I thought Zack would be far more romance minded. How many times has he swept you off your feet now?"

"Including third grade?" Kelly thought a moment. "At least seven times."

"And counting," Jessie added.

Kelly's smile faded. "No, I think seven times is more than enough. I've learned my lesson where Zack is concerned."

"It probably isn't any of my business," Jessie said, "but Zack is really nuts about you. I know he's kind of lost track of that a couple of times—"

"Like any time a pretty girl walked by or there was a scam to be scammed," Kelly pointed out.

"—but he always came back to you," Jessie finished.

Kelly tossed her hair over her shoulder. "Well, maybe I don't want him to come back to me anymore. In fact, I think the more guys I date, the more I'll find Zack Morris was just a phase I was going through. Binky Grayson was flirting with me the other day. At least, I think he was, even if he was talking about caviar. He's really nice and knows everyone who's anyone in Palisades. And what do you think about Vance Hemmelstein? He tripped on the steps at school when I said hi to him today. He's awfully cute, and he drives that really cool classic 'vette."

▲   ▼   ▲

Outside Kelly's window, Zack nearly lost his grip and fell off the porch roof. Vance Hemmelstein! The guy played a trombone in the marching band, collected bottle caps, and in the local surfing tournament held the last week of summer had washed ashore two feet ahead of his surfboard. Kelly couldn't be serious about dating Vance!

He wished he'd never decided to follow Jessie. This wasn't the kind of information he wanted to gather.

"So, has Binky or Vance asked you out yet?" Jessie demanded.

"Not yet," Kelly admitted. "But they will if I want them to."

Zack gritted his teeth and tried to inch closer to hear more.

"Are you really going to enter the video contest, Jessie?" Kelly asked.

Ah! Now here was what he'd scaled the porch to hear, Zack thought.

"I have to," Jessie said. "And I want you to help me show that narrow-minded Neanderthal that I was right."

"Gosh! I'd love to help, but didn't you promise you wouldn't enter?"

"I've been thinking about that," Jessie admitted. "First, I can't be held accountable for the oath I signed since it was done under duress."

"You didn't have to do it," Kelly said. "I told you not to. Remember?"

"I couldn't back down. Not to Slater and Zack of all people. Besides, if I remember the wording right, I only said that I had no ulterior motives in offering my help—and I didn't, at least not concerning entering the contest myself—and that I would not pick up a camera to film my own video. That's where you come in."

"Me?" Kelly squeaked.

"I need you to hold the camera. That way I can produce a video without breaking any of those promises I made," Jessie explained.

Zack cringed. Talk about leaving loopholes! He'd left Jessie one big enough to jump a circus elephant through! It was time to scratch "lawyer" off his list of future careers. If things went well on his current covert operation, though, he could replace it with "secret agent" easily. No sweat.

"Do you have a theme in mind?" Kelly asked.

"Absolutely," Jessie assured her. "I think that this film clip should be aimed at a certain type of tourist, a type that is overlooked by the usual tourist hype."

Zack inched closer to the window. A little brown

bird fluttered nearby and took up a position where he could watch both Zack spread-eagled against the back porch roof and the girls inside Kelly's room.

"There are a lot of people who are conscious about what they eat these days," Jessie explained. "They buy organically raised food, especially fruits and vegetables. A lot of these people are vegetarians like me. I think a video concentrating on organic farms nearby and our quality vegetarian restaurants could tap a whole new tourist market. What do you think?"

"I think it's nuts," Zack told the little bird. "What about you?"

His feathered friend cocked his head to one side as if considering.

"Give me a burger any day," Zack said to the bird.

"I really value your opinion, Kelly," Jessie continued, "because you've taken acting classes, had that chance to be on television, and can give me a valuable contribution."

"And I can run the camera," Kelly reminded her. "I don't know, Jessie. Scholarship money is scholarship money, but this means more to Slater than just that."

"I know."

"Still, you were only trying to help him, and he was being pig-headed."

"To put it lightly," Jessie agreed.

Kelly was silent a moment longer as she considered.

Zack raised his head slightly to peer inside the room.

"Okay," Kelly announced. "I'll do it. When do we start filming?"

"How about now?" Jessie asked. "I brought the video camera with me because we can get a great shot of Mr. Petrovsky's artichoke field from your window."

From the window? Zack gulped, and scooted hastily toward the drainpipe. He fell out of sight a millisecond before the girls had the camera running.

Chapter 6

▲ ▼ ▲ ▼ ▲

His parents' video camera held to his eye, Slater scanned the beach, zeroing in on a couple of really cute girls who were tossing a large, colorful, inflated ball back and forth. "This was a great idea, preppie," he declared.

Zack leaned back in the sand, sunglasses resting low on his nose. The weather had been perfect for two days. Which made for a couple of the longest school days in history. Both days he and Slater had jumped in his car after the last bell and made good use of the daylight to shoot film footage. The beach was his favorite location so far, Zack decided as he watched a couple of laughing girls stroll by.

"What else do we need to shoot while we're here?" Zack asked.

"Can't think of anything," Slater said. "We got

the volleyball game, the Frisbee game, the sun-bathers, the sand castle builders, the swimmers, the surfers, and even a couple of snorkelers." He finished his shot and turned the camera off. Being extremely careful to keep sand out of it, he eased the camera back into its protective case. "My big question is, do we have any chili dogs left?"

"Just one." Zack hastily finished off a can of soda. "But we're fresh out of cold drinks."

Slater dropped down next to him and bit into the chili dog. "I think we've kept things fairly even on this video," he admitted. "I mean, when we did cheer-leader shots, we included the guys on the football team in a lineup; when we did girls in tennis shorts, we included lifeguards at the club pool; and we were even more balanced here at the beach, keeping the number of hunks and babes exactly the same."

"Right. There is no way anyone can say this video was made by a sexist pig," Zack said.

"Except for Jessie," Slater reminded his friend and associate producer.

"Forget Jessie. With the lame idea she's working on, this contest is in the bag," Zack said.

"Yeah, but for who?" Slater asked. "What if the judges are all vegetarian old maids who hate sports and long-legged girls?"

Zack slid his sunglasses back in place and lay back in the sand, his hands behind his head. "Who could possibly hate long-legged girls?"

"Ms. Martinet," Slater said.

Ms. Martinet had been the temporary principal at Bayside High for a short time and had tried to run the school like a prisoner-of-war camp. Miniskirts had been at the top of her long list of things to wipe from the face of the earth.

"You would have to ruin a perfectly good day by bringing her up," Zack groaned.

Slater finished off his chili dog and stretched out to catch a few rays himself. "What's next on the shooting schedule?"

"Rollerblading, I think," Zack said after a moment of thought. "Then maybe an aerobics class at the community center. Both high-quality forms of local entertainment."

"The finest," Slater agreed. He gazed up at the sky and then out at the waves as they washed up on the beach. This was what made Palisades a great place to live. After all the places he'd lived as his family moved from one military base to another, Slater figured he knew a terrific location when he saw one. If anyone could get that point across to visitors, A. C. Slater was the one to do it.

At least he thought he was. Still, one of Jessie's comments nagged at him.

"Zack? You know, everything we've filmed today is stuff that you can find in other California coastal towns."

"Yeah," Zack agreed. "Great, isn't it?"

"For us, it is," Slater said. "But why would a tourist pick Palisades as a vacation spot rather than, say, San Diego?"

"We're a smaller, more friendly community."

"Long Beach is more centrally located to places like the movie studios and Disneyland."

"With the freeway system, so are we, and our air is cleaner since we're farther away from Los Angeles," Zack said. "Besides, people from large cities like to vacation in smaller towns."

"Why pick Palisades over a place like Morro Bay then?" Slater asked. "I visited my grandfather there once. It's a tiny place, the view is great, the waves are wonderful, and the people are friendly."

"Too far north to include the LA sights," Zack declared smoothly. "Palisades is perfect, and your video is going to show the best of what we have to offer."

Slater stared out to sea. "I don't know. I'd feel much more confident if I knew for sure what Jessie was doing. What if the girls saw you outside Kelly's window and just made up all that stuff about organic farms and vegetarian restaurants?"

"Mmm. Maybe I should do some more espionage work," Zack mused.

"Only this time, don't try to be a human fly. Just ask Kelly out and get her to talk about what Jessie's doing," Slater suggested.

"Mmm," Zack mumbled. "Only one problem with that. I can't ask Kelly out if I'm broke."

Slater shifted in the sand. "How can you be broke? I just lent you ten bucks two days ago. What did you spend it on?"

"That's *who*, not what," Zack corrected. "When I fell off the roof at Kelly's house, her little sister Erin saw me. I had to shell out hush money and do it fast before Jessie and Kelly saw me."

"Erin's only ten," Slater said. "A buck would seem like a lot of money to her."

"Ha! You don't know Erin Kapowski very well, do you? That kid is into high finance. I had to cough up five bucks or else."

"Five dollars? Didn't you try to talk her down?"

"That *was* talking her down," Zack assured him. "Erin wanted twenty-five."

Slater heaved a big sigh and dug in the pocket of his shorts. "You're lucky I'm not dating anybody right now or I wouldn't be able to finance your social life."

"Then don't think of it as my social life," Zack recommended, whisking a ten out of Slater's hand. "If you want me to pump Kelly for information on Jessie's project, it's going to cost more than this. I'll pay you back."

Slater's eyes narrowed. "What are you planning to do? Dazzle her with a romantic dinner and dancing?"

Zack thought about the earlier part of the girls' conversation, the part where Kelly insisted Slater was a more romantic date than he was. What about all those moonlit nights at the beach? All that hand-holding and tender kissing? Weren't all those times they'd spent together romantic?

"Dinner and dancing, huh? Is that what you did with Kelly when you dated her?" Zack asked.

Slater shrugged. "Once, I guess. Mostly we just sat and talked, walked on the beach, stuff like that."

So what made that more romantic than an evening with Zack Morris? Zack wondered. Well, there was only one way to find out, and that was to ask someone. Not Kelly, of course, but someone. Lisa, maybe. She dated so many different guys she was sure to know what was romantic and what wasn't. And why something was romantic with one person and not with another. But just in case, he would do well to be prepared.

Zack held out his hand. "Another twenty ought to take care of expenses. You want this espionage work done right, don't you, Slater?"

▲   ▼   ▲

Kelly sat in the darkened front room of the Spano home and watched the television screen. She and Jessie had gotten some really great shots of Mr. Petrovsky's artichoke plants and one of his cute son checking the irrigation system. When Pavel's handsome features flashed into view, Kelly sighed happily.

"So, what do you think?" Jessie demanded as the film clip finished off. "Pretty comprehensive so far, isn't it?"

"Wellll," Kelly answered a bit reluctantly. "It

does remind me a bit of those documentary shows on public television."

Jessie smiled brightly. "It does? That's great!"

"Uh, yeah," Kelly agreed, far from enthusiastic. "It's great if that's what you want. But if I were a tourist watching this, I wouldn't come to Palisades for my vacation."

Jessie's smile vanished. "You wouldn't? Oh, but that's because you aren't a vegetarian."

"No, I think it's because even if I were a vegetarian I'd want to do more than eat organic food while visiting Palisades."

"Oh." Jessie sank down into the cushions of the sofa. "Then let's go at this a different way. When you do pick a place to go on vacation, what are you looking for?"

"Me?" Kelly pondered a moment. "Well, I've never actually gotten to pick a place to go before. Mom and Dad do that. What would you look for? Other than organic vegetarian restaurants."

"That's easy," Jessie announced. "I'd want to go someplace where there were lots of museums, plenty of history, and libraries galore."

"You would?" Kelly didn't sound thrilled. "What about amusement parks, beaches, and boys?"

"I've got that here, Kel. Why would I want to do those things while on vacation? Do you have something else in mind?"

Kelly sighed and pushed back into the sofa cushions, snuggling deep into the softness. "Well, yeah. I'd like to have a wonderfully romantic time with a gorgeous guy. In fact, I think that's why your video is boring. It needs to show that Palisades is a place where people fall in love."

"Love?" Jessie laughed. "That's really hokey, Kelly. Now, tell me what you really think."

Insulted that Jessie wasn't taking her suggestion seriously, Kelly sat up straighter, no longer relaxed. "That is what I *really* think. Your video is great if you want to know about growing artichokes without pesticides, but terrible if you're trying to convince people they should come to Palisades on vacation. Since that's the object of the contest, I think you need to show Palisades is romantic. As well," she added in an apologetic voice as Jessie began to grind her teeth.

"So you want me to make my entry the same old hash that everyone else's will be, is that it?" Jessie demanded.

"Similar, perhaps, but not the same," Kelly said. "You're doing this because you wanted to show Slater that he wasn't doing as convincing a project as he could, right?"

Jessie made a noise that could have been either agreement or a growl.

"Well, I'm just doing the same for you," Kelly said.

"So you think my idea stinks," Jessie said.

"I didn't say that. It's just that . . ."

"It stinks," Jessie repeated.

"Well, yes," Kelly admitted.

"What you're saying is that, creatively, you and I don't see eye to eye on this," Jessie persisted.

"You could say that."

"And we never will see eye to eye on it."

"Well, yes," Kelly said slowly.

"So we would do better not to continue this partnership," Jessie declared. "You can just go off and make your own video. After all, you could use the scholarship money just as much as the rest of us."

"More so," Kelly murmured under her breath. She was the one with six brothers and sisters. All her friends were only children who wouldn't be paying their own way to college as she had to.

Jessie held out her hand. "May the best woman win," she said.

Kelly hadn't planned on entering the contest. With her friends so determined to win, she would have to be crazy to try to make her own video. But Jessie's attitude was enough to make anyone crazy.

Kelly slapped her hand in Jessie's and shook it. "May the best woman win," she agreed. "But it's going to be me this time, Jessie. Me."

Chapter 7

▲ ▼ ▲ ▼ ▲

Zack checked his hair one last time before climbing out of his classic '65 Mustang convertible and heading for the front door of the Kapowski house. He was still a little stunned over how fast Kelly had agreed to go out with him. He had expected to have to talk her into the date, to lie and say he just wanted to see her as a friend. It wasn't that much of a lie. She was his friend. He just wanted her to be his girl as well.

Her cheerful acceptance of his offer to take her to the movies must mean that Kelly missed him as much as he missed her. Seeing each other every day at school didn't count. It wasn't as if he talked to her on the phone every night as he'd once done. It wasn't as if she let him pick her up and drive her to school in the morning and home again in the afternoon. It wasn't as if she held hands with him and gazed happily into his eyes.

Those were all things a guy really missed once he didn't have them. It would be wonderful to be back together again.

Of course, she could have accepted just because she didn't have another date and didn't want to stay home on a Friday night.

Zack decided he'd take his chances.

He'd come prepared with fresh ammunition. A consultation with Lisa had given him a whole new outlook on this romance thing.

Romance, Lisa claimed, wasn't just spending time with a great-looking guy.

That bit of information had floored him.

Romance, Lisa said, was something you had to work at.

Ouch!

Romance meant that when you were alone with a girl and the moonlight was bright, the night was warm, the surf was up, and you gazed into her eyes you actually listened to what she was saying.

Double ouch!

Romance was when you invited a girl out, you asked what she wanted to do, what movie she wanted to see, what food she wanted to eat. And then you did what she wanted.

So much for a Roller Derby game and a pizza with anchovies!

To win Kelly back, though, Zack was willing to endure it all. He was going to discover what was important to her, eat at the little French bistro she had always wanted to try, and watch the latest Mitch Tobias movie. He'd even try not to flinch when she sighed over the handsome actor.

Now that was devotion.

And, if he was lucky, he'd even find out how production was going on Jessie's video.

That was a minor consideration, even if Slater was bankrolling this date. A man had to follow his own dream, after all.

Ten-year-old Erin answered the door when he knocked.

"Kelly knows I'm supposed to be here," Zack assured the little girl quickly, before she could have her hand out for another donation.

"Okay," Erin said. "I can wait till you bring her home and want me to get lost. It costs more than a dollar now, though."

"You'll be lucky to get fifty cents more out of me," Zack snarled. "What I should do is tell your mom that you're up past your bedtime."

Erin gave him a smile that showed missing teeth. "If you do, I'll tell Kerry that you want to kiss Kelly," she threatened. Kerry was one of their older brothers.

"Kerry knows I want to kiss Kelly," Zack said smugly.

"But he doesn't like it," Erin informed him. She giggled when Zack looked a bit worried.

Fortunately for Zack, Kelly skipped down the stairs at that moment.

She looked wonderful, her brightly colored sundress setting off the warm tone of her tanned skin. Her toenails were polished a fire-engine red and peeked out from wispy little sandals.

"Hi!" she greeted, her voice a bit breathless, as if she had been running. Or maybe she was excited to see him. "I can't believe that we're actually going to see Mitch's new movie!"

Zack hated the intimate sound of the actor's name on her lips. If he had paid more attention to Kelly when they visited New York City on a class trip, Kelly never would have met the handsome actor. The guy had been nothing more than a cab driver then. Now he was on the way to being a big Hollywood box office star.

"What's it called again?" Zack asked.

"*Paradise in His Arms,*" Kelly said, and sighed happily. "Mitch is this sea captain and . . ."

Zack tuned out. According to Lisa's instructions, he needed to really listen to what Kelly said, but that didn't necessarily include thumbnail sketches of movies. Did it?

"It should be really neat," Kelly gushed. "In an interview I saw on *Entertainment Beat,* Mitch said it was awesome to film. He even did his own stunts!"

What a guy! Zack hated him more every minute.

"I just know I'll break out in a sweat when he inches out on that yardarm to cut a crew member free from the ropes during a storm. Mitch says he thinks the shots look really believable since they were actually at sea when those scenes were filmed," Kelly babbled on.

Zack held up a hand. "Don't tell me another thing," he urged. "I don't want anything to spoil my enjoyment of the movie."

Kelly twinkled up at him. "Oh, I'm so glad you're taking me to see it," she said, and took Zack's arm. "I don't think I could enjoy it as much with anyone else."

Well, that was encouraging. Zack's chest expanded with pride.

"I called Mitch to tell him I was going to see his movie tonight, and he told me to call back the minute I got home to tell him what I thought of it," Kelly said.

Air whistled through Zack's teeth as his ego deflated like a punctured balloon.

"Mitch wants to know what you think, too, Zack," Kelly assured him. "He wants to find out what guys think of his movies. He would like to appeal to a wide audience and not just be a heartthrob like Errol Flynn was."

"Who?"

Kelly giggled. "He was the movie star my grandmother had this really bad crush on when she was my age," she explained.

Sort of like the one Kelly seemed to have on Mitch Tobias? The trouble was, Kelly knew Mitch personally. Not only from riding in his cab in New York City, but from the acting class he'd taught in California. Mitch had introduced her to his agent, who had gotten Kelly a job in a commercial and also sent her on an audition for another one.

Mitch Tobias was tough competition for any guy determined to make a steady place for himself in Kelly's life.

"Hey, great!" Zack declared with a false smile. "I'm sure I'll like this flick, though."

"I'm sure you will, too," Kelly said, and tugged him out the door. "But if we don't hurry, we'll miss the opening credits."

"We certainly wouldn't want to do that," Zack said. He was glad Kelly was already three steps ahead of him so she didn't see that he wasn't as thrilled as she was. *Paradise in His Arms*. Zack cringed just thinking about the title. He hoped that none of the guys at school ever found out he'd gone to see it.

This romance stuff was harder than Lisa had made it sound. But for Kelly . . .

She turned around to face him when she reached the Mustang. The evening breeze tossed her veil of long dark hair, lifting it from her shoulders. The full skirt of her dress swirled around her legs.

The stars seemed to dance in her eyes as she grinned at him.

Zack squared his shoulders. *Mitch Tobias, here I come*, he thought. *Ready or not*.

▲   ▼   ▲

Kelly sniffled for the fifth time and, using Zack's handkerchief, blew her nose. On the wide screen, Mitch Tobias gazed down into the face of a pretty strawberry blond actress, telling her how much he'd tried to ignore her, to forget her. Kelly hiccupped softly as tears rolled down her face.

"Oh, Zack," she whispered. "Isn't it sad? And so wonderful, too?"

Zack took a chance. He put his arm around Kelly's shoulders and cuddled her close. He was pleased when her head settled against his chest and her hand gripped his. Her eyes were still on Mitch in the movie, but Zack felt a lot better.

The movie wasn't as bad as he'd feared. There were some really neat fight sequences, and the rescue in the rigging had been thrilling. The best part had been when Kelly accepted his handkerchief, his shoulder, and murmured his name, though.

Letting her pick the movie hadn't been such a dumb idea after all.

By the time the final credits rolled, Kelly was mopping her eyes and grinning happily at him.

"Thank you, Zack. This was a very special evening," she said. "I'll never forget it."

"It doesn't have to be over yet," Zack offered. "We could grab something to eat."

"At the Max I suppose," Kelly said. She didn't sound overly enthusiastic.

"Or someplace else," Zack said hastily. He didn't want this evening to end too soon. Especially since it would be over the minute Kelly placed her collect call to Mitch. Collect, for goodness sakes! That didn't sit well with a guy who'd had to borrow money to take her to see the movie.

"I'm not really hungry," Kelly admitted. "Not after all that popcorn. Maybe we could just take a walk on the beach."

Zack knew just the stop. Their special place. What could be more romantic? The moon was silvery, the night was balmy, and the sea would whisper the same music they'd heard in the movie.

Uh-oh. Bad move.

"How does that sound?" Kelly asked.

"Uh, great. Great. But I really need something to wash all that popcorn down," Zack said, and guided her out of the theater and into the parking lot. "I'll just stop by the Max and get something to go."

"Oh, don't bother, Zack. You've been so sweet to me tonight, the least I can do is raid the refrigerator at home to feed you," Kelly said.

That didn't sound very romantic, but maybe he shouldn't rush into things too quickly. It would be better to do this by stages. All he had to do was not look at other girls, listen to what Kelly said, do what Kelly wanted, and sooner or later she'd be back in his arms for good.

Excellent plan, Zack decided. Kelly wouldn't get suspicious, and in the end she'd fall back in love with him. Most excellent plan.

And speaking of plans, he still had to find out what Jessie was up to on her video for the contest.

"You know," Zack said as he settled behind the wheel of his car. "Watching that movie made me wonder what kind of stuff the Channel 17 judges will be viewing when the videos are all turned in on Monday. I'd sure hate to have to decide on a winner."

"Yeah," Kelly agreed. "It should be tough. I'll bet there are a lot of kids entering. The scholarship money is really great."

Well, that didn't tell him anything. Zack decided to try a new tack.

"Do you think Slater has a chance?"

Kelly considered the matter carefully. "This is his second year in broadcasting. Last year was pretty basic stuff, but they're doing more advanced work this year. I think he'll do well."

"As well as some of the other entries? I wonder what kind of subjects are being filmed? I mean," Zack added, trying to sound nonchalant rather than desperate, "there are so many great topics someone could do on Palisades. Like . . ." He searched his mind for something unrelated to Slater's video that was likely to interest Jessie. "Oh, say, like history."

Kelly wrinkled her nose. "Ugh. That doesn't sound very exciting to me. You sound more like Jessie, Zack."

Ah!

"I do?"

"She claims that in picking a vacation spot she'd look for a place stuffed with museums."

"Ugh."

Kelly beamed at him. "That's what I say. Ugh!"

Time for Plan C.

"I heard Slater and Jessie had an argument over his idea," Zack said.

"So what's new? Slater and Jessie always argue."

Zack tried again. "Do you know what it was about?"

Kelly shrugged. "Oh, the usual with them. Jessie was trying to improve on Slater's idea, and he didn't like her suggestions."

That much he already knew. Zack tried to think of another comment to make, something that would head Kelly in the direction he needed her to go. Before he came up with a brainstorm, Kelly sighed.

"You know, I really understand how Jessie felt. But she's no better at taking suggestions than Slater is. I offered her a bit of advice, and she got all huffy. Jessie just doesn't take constructive criticism well."

This sounded good.

"That's too bad. I know you only had the best of

intentions," Zack soothed. "What would you have done to improve her video?"

Kelly giggled. "Dump everything except the clip of Pavel Petrovsky."

Pavel Petr— Zack swallowed loudly. Pavel was what girls called a hunk and a half. He was tall, muscle-bound, and had a mass of curly black hair and dimples that were even more devastating than Slater's.

Of course, the Petrovsky name alone was enough to tell him that he hadn't heard wrong when he was on Kelly's roof. Jessie was concentrating on arti-chokes and their green and leafy friends. Talk about a real snoozer of a show!

"I really had a nice time tonight, Zack," Kelly said as he pulled his car up before her house. "Thank you for taking me to the show."

Because she'd been weeping through most of the movie, her eyes were even more star drenched than before. The breeze wafted the scent of her perfume to him.

"I'm glad we went, too," Zack confessed. "I really enjoyed it. But I don't think it was the movie so much as the company."

Kelly's long lashes dipped to hide her eyes. "Oh, Zack," she whispered before looking back up at him.

"I've missed being with you, Kelly. I miss sharing with you, talking to you. I miss just looking at you. You're so pretty. Especially tonight."

"I've missed you, too," she admitted. "We've

been friends for so long—"

Zack laid a finger against her lips, halting her speech. "We are good friends, Kelly. We have been for a long time. Will be for even longer, I hope."

"Oh, Zack, of course—"

"Hush," he murmured. Gently Zack brushed his lips against hers. When she didn't pull away, he nearly sighed in relief. As tempting as it was to kiss her again, he wasn't going to rush her. He knew too well that Kelly might not believe he was serious about her. This time he wasn't just going to tell her he loved her—he was going to show her he did.

Zack leaned back in his seat. "You'd better go in before Kerry decides to come out and rip my head off."

She giggled again. "He wouldn't do that, silly. Besides, I still owe you a snack."

"I think I'll pass on the food. I'm taking no chances with Kerry," Zack said. "Would you like to do something together tomorrow?"

"That would be nice," Kelly said, "but I can't. You see, I've decided to film my own video and enter the scholarship contest. I've got a lot of work to do if I'm going to make the deadline!"

Chapter 8

▲ ▼ ▲ ▼ ▲

Kelly felt wonderful when she woke up the next morning. After saying good-night to Zack, she'd called Mitch and given him a glowing review of the movie. He'd laughed and said he should have known better than to ask her opinion. He had been pleased to hear that Zack hadn't been totally grossed out by it, and he'd been really interested when she told him about the contest video. Mitch had even told her to give him a call if she needed any help with it.

It was nice to have friends outside of those at school. Still, she'd never find better friends than the ones at Bayside.

And handsome and nice as Mitch was, he wasn't someone she knew all that well. Not like any of the gang. Not like Zack.

Kelly wandered over to the window seat in her

room and plunked down on the cushions. The day was lovely. There was a blue sky overhead and a balmy breeze stirring the branches of the trees in the Kapowskis' yard. She could hear the happy squeals of her little brother, Billy, and her youngest sister, Erin, as they played on the jungle gym set out back. Rather than watch them, Kelly stared out over the neighboring artichoke field and thought about her video.

What would best show that Palisades was a wonderful place for people in love to visit? she wondered.

Too bad she wasn't in love at the moment. Well, not totally. There had always been a soft spot in her heart for Zack. Even though being just friends with him had been more her idea than his, there were still times when she was really tempted to get back together with him.

Especially after a wonderful evening like the one they had spent together last night.

Zack had been so . . . so . . . different! He'd actually taken her to a show she wanted to see and hadn't said anything derogatory about it, either during the movie or after. He'd asked her what *she* wanted to do. He hadn't just dragged her along.

Even the fact that he'd foregone a stop at the Max was awesome.

And when he'd kissed her, oh so lightly . . .

Kelly closed her eyes, tilted her chin up, and remembered that soft butterfly-light caress. She sighed. Now *that* had been romantic.

Maybe she and Zack . . .

The sound of the back door banging shut brought Kelly out of her daydream. What was she thinking? She'd had about a zillion reasons for breaking up with Zack. All of them good reasons. Very good reasons. Zack might seem as if he was changing—for the better—but one lovely evening didn't mean that things would continue to be wonderful if they became a couple again.

Besides, knowing Zack, he probably had a reason for behaving differently. He'd lulled her into being at ease with him, lulled her into remembering the good times with him.

There was probably a scam behind it, Kelly admitted to herself. She'd known Zack Morris too long not to know the way he worked.

And Zack was smoothest when a scam was in progress.

What had they talked about? Spanish class, the latest rumors around school, the outcome of last week's ball game, the movie, Jessie and Slater's latest disagreement, the size of the moon . . .

Wait! Jessie and Slater! That was it!

Kelly wrapped her arms around her updrawn legs and rested her chin on her knees. She smiled secretly to herself. Zack had guided the conversation around to Jessie's video. He'd been trying to find out what she was working on!

Kelly's grin widened. That meant Slater had sent

Zack to ferret out information. He was worried that Jessie would beat him in the contest.

Until Zack told him, Slater wouldn't even know he had other competition among his friends. Competition that had just as much experience in filmmaking as he had.

Heck, she had more experience, Kelly decided. After all, she had been the Piglet Pop Princess in an advertising campaign and almost had a speaking part in commercials for Uncle Sam's Hamburger Haven. She'd also taken acting classes. Sure, she'd never actually handled a camera before and her family didn't even own one, but those were trivial things. They wouldn't slow her down.

The first thing to do was decide on her concept, what she wanted to include, how she wanted to present it, and then . . . then she'd worry about where to borrow a video camera.

A little dream formed in her head. Kelly could see herself, in a dazzling silver evening gown, accepting the scholarship award and the praises of the contest judges for her brilliant film.

"The most moving five minutes I've ever experienced," a woman judge in a large pink flowered hat told her, pressing Kelly's hand ardently.

"I foresee a wonderful future for you, young lady," a man in a business suit said, his eyes misty with emotion.

"If only you could work with the Visitors Bureau

rather than go to school," a third judge murmured, "we would be able to revise our whole promotion concept."

Kelly saw herself smiling widely as she stepped down from the podium only to be rushed by a crowd of people anxious for her autograph.

"Hey, Kelly!" Erin yelled, opening Kelly's bedroom door.

"Of course, I'll be glad to sign your book," Kelly said, still in her dream world.

"You okay, Kel? You look kind of weird," Erin said.

As if it were a giant pink bubble, Kelly's dream popped. "I was just thinking," she murmured.

Erin wrinkled her nose. "About that dopey Zack, I'll bet," she declared with ten-year-old disdain. "Mom wants you to run to the store for some milk while she fixes lunch."

Kelly got to her feet and found her purse. "I was not," she said. "Besides, Zack isn't dopey."

At least, most of the time he wasn't. He would sure look that way when she trounced everyone in the video contest, though, Kelly decided smugly.

What a switch this was! Kelly Kapowski pulling a scam on Zack Morris.

This was most certainly one for the Bayside history books.

▲　▼　▲

Slater was surprised but pleased when his father

took a seat in the family room and watched Slater's contest entry with him. Major Slater was so busy at the military base that he was frequently unavailable for sharing things with his son. He tried to make it to the Bayside football games to watch A. C. quarterback the plays, but he frequently missed most of the game. He tried to rearrange his schedule to attend the wrestling meets A. C. competed in, but government business often pulled him out of town when championship events occurred. Slater had gotten so used to his father not being around to share in his interests that having the major there to watch the film made him even more proud of the job he'd done on it.

When the television screen went blank, Major Slater's hand fell on A. C.'s shoulder in a grip of approval. "You did a really fine job," he told his son. "As much as I'd like you to follow in my footsteps, I can see that you've developed quite a talent for filmmaking."

Slater grinned widely at his father's praise. "Thanks, Dad. Of course, I'm more interested in being a sports broadcaster, but knowing how to put together a film clip is just as important."

The major nodded. "Diversification. An excellent plan. Knowing how important your career ambitions are, I did a little investigating on my own."

Slater's mouth nearly dropped open. "You did?"

His father laughed. "You have every right to be

surprised. I wasn't very supportive when you first mentioned going into broadcasting."

Slater shrugged. "Because I'm breaking rank in not following the family tradition of pursuing a military career," he mumbled.

"I've been trying to see your side, A. C.," the major insisted. "So I had one of my aides gather information about the best broadcasting programs available in universities across the country and around the world."

Around the world? Slater felt a knot form in his stomach. He'd lived so many places in his life, that mention of any country other than the good old U.S.A. made him nervous.

His father was excited, though. There was nothing he loved more than the thrill of visiting a new place, of taking a new assignment. Major Slater thrived on travel; A. C. hated it. But he'd never let his dad know how he felt.

"Look at these," the major urged, handing Slater a handful of brochures. "I think you'll be impressed. I certainly was. This is the top gun of all broadcasting schools."

Slater stared at the cover of the first brochure. It showed a modern building, six stories tall, made of concrete and steel and glass. The size of it dwarfed the mature shade trees at its base and made the students milling on the quad look small and insignificant.

So far so good. At least it wasn't an ivy-covered mausoleum from the Middle Ages as he'd feared. When his father mentioned the world at large, Slater worried that he was headed for an ancient university in Europe. This wasn't ancient, it was modern. It looked like the kind of place that would have the most up-to-date equipment. It actually looked pretty interesting.

Or it did until he noticed the name of the school.

"Houndslow Heath University School of Broadcasting," Slater read out loud, his voice nearly choked with dread. "Dad, that's in London. In England."

The major beamed happily at him. "Yes. Isn't it great? It's a tough school to get admitted to, but I know you can pass the entrance tests, son. This video you've done about Palisades will carry a good bit of weight, if I'm any judge. And I can always pull a few strings, call in a few favors people owe me, and smooth the whole process for you. I'll put in for reassignment to England and . . ."

Slater let his father continue to enthuse over his plan. To cover his own lack of enthusiasm, Slater leafed through the brochures. Houndslow Heath was indeed an elite school for anyone interested in a career in broadcasting. Instructors there ranged from retired news professionals in the world of print journalism as well as radio and television, to men and women currently employed by various award-winning British broadcasting companies. There were Americans on the staff, Germans, French, Brazilians, Japanese—every nation appeared to be represented to give students a global outlook on broadcasting.

If he wanted nothing more than a job in broadcasting, the school was perfect, Slater realized.

But he wanted more than just that. He wanted a permanent place in the world, somewhere he belonged, where he was a part of things.

It was something his father would never understand.

Major Slater continued to talk happily about the opportunities A. C. would have with a degree from Houndslow Heath U. He reminded his son of the beautiful green countryside they'd enjoyed when stationed in England before, of the friends A. C. had made there.

"And now that you're older, travel on the Continent will interest you more than it did when you were younger," the major said. "Remember the holidays when we'd take off and explore the beaches of the Riviera or do a bit of skiing in the Alps?"

"Yeah. Great idea, Dad," Slater declared, trying to sound excited about the prospect.

The major leaned back in his chair and put his feet up. "It will be great to pack up the family again," he said. "We've been in Palisades for quite a while now. Almost long enough to put down roots." He chuckled as if he'd made a joke.

Almost? Slater echoed to himself. He had put them down, had sunk them deep into the California soil. He had friends here, good friends. He was important at Bayside in a way he'd never been at any of the other schools he'd attended while his father dragged them around the world.

It was true he wanted to be a broadcaster. But he wanted to be one here—in the U.S.A.—in California. He wanted a hometown for once in his life. And he wanted it to be Palisades.

But he also didn't want to hurt his dad's feelings. The major had made an effort to be more involved in his life, and Slater didn't want to let him down.

Well, there was still plenty of time before he had to make a decision. There was always a chance that Houndslow Heath wouldn't accept him. There was always a chance that the Bayside gang would be split up when they went to college anyway. If everyone was leaving, would he still want to stay in Palisades?

The best thing he could do was keep an open mind about his father's plan. All he had to do was act enthusiastic for the major's sake.

He might not have the benefit of Kelly's acting lessons, but Slater was fairly sure he could pretend to be excited.

"So, what do you think?" the major asked.

Slater cleared the lump of despair that was lodged in his throat. "I think it all sounds great, Dad," he declared with a forced smile.

This acting business was harder than he'd thought. But as long as he didn't hurt his father's feelings, the effort would be worth it.

At least Slater sure hoped it would.

Chapter 9

▲ ▼ ▲ ▼ ▲

Lisa leaned forward in her chair, giving her whole attention to the film that played on the television in the Turtles' front room.

Next to her, perched on the very edge of another chair, Jessie waited anxiously for the video to play out. Her hazel eyes flitted back and forth between Lisa and the screen.

It took all of Lisa's self-control to remain calm under her friend's gaze. Especially when Lisa would have preferred to shut her eyes rather than watch the eight-minute-long tour of Palisades' vegetarian restaurants.

At long last the screen flickered and went to black. Lisa leaned back in her seat and searched madly for something nice to say about her friend's film work.

Jessie hit the rewind button on the remote control.

Lisa hoped that didn't mean she had to watch the video a second time. Once was bad enough.

"Well?" Jessie asked eagerly. "What do you think?"

"Very nice, girlfriend," Lisa said. "There are some especially nice changes in angle that are . . ." She searched about frantically for an appropriate word. ". . . that are, well, intriguing is probably the best way to describe them."

Jessie glowed with approval. "Really? That's great! Which one in particular caught your eye?"

Eww, Lisa thought. She'd known she was in trouble the moment a shot of an artichoke had flickered to life on the television set. This was going to be tough to critique without hurting Jessie's feelings.

Lisa leaned back so that she was staring at the ceiling rather than her friend's anxious face. Now if only she could find inspiration there. The paint was a series of swirls that looked like seashells. There had been nothing about the ocean in Jessie's video. No luck there. The ceiling fan made lazy swishes above them, barely stirring the air. The blades whirled by, a blur of darker color against the white ceiling.

A blur! That was it.

"Well, there was that one shot early on," Lisa said. "The angle of the frame was just out of kilter enough to be really artistic, and the fact that the focus was blurred before it clarified was very . . . er, artistic, too."

Jessie relaxed back in her seat. "You mean the shot of the field? We were going to take that from Kelly's bedroom window. Then we decided we'd get a wider view if Kelly climbed out onto the porch roof. She slipped a bit and slid down the shingles. That's why the angle is crooked and the frame is out of focus."

"Oh," Lisa said.

"I was going to take it out, but if you think it's artistic, maybe I'd better leave it in."

Lisa searched for another avenue to take and came up with a big zero. "You were going to cut that?" she asked, hoping to gain time.

Jessie sighed. "I have to cut something. The video is a lot longer than the contest rules allow. But it's all so good, I can't decide which bits to kill. I was hoping you'd have some suggestions."

The best suggestion she could give, Lisa mused, was to forget the whole thing. She'd never been so bored with a show in her whole life!

"Maybe some of the restaurant scenes," she offered in desperation. "I didn't realize there were quite so many vegetarian and health food restaurants in Palisades."

"Amazing, isn't it?" Jessie agreed happily. "And everyone was so kind and helpful about letting me into their kitchens to film."

Lisa nodded. "Yes, I've never seen squash and artichokes fixed in so many different ways before," she said. "Perhaps if you . . ."

"And then service is so important," Jessie continued. "I couldn't neglect that aspect of each place. And there is atmosphere to consider."

"Atmosphere," Lisa repeated with a nod. Actually all the places had looked fairly alike to her. They favored rough board siding and a country motif. The only tablecloths she'd noticed had been either red check or blue check.

"So you can see where I'm having trouble," Jessie said. "What I want you to do is tell me how you'd fix it if it was your video." Jessie grinned and reached forward to pick up a notebook and pencil. "I know I can trust you, Lisa. Unlike Kelly, you aren't planning on entering the contest."

"No way," Lisa assured her. "I've got more than I can handle keeping up with all the sales at the mall."

Jessie tapped the pencil on her paper. "So. What would you do if this was your video?"

Lisa tapped one finger thoughtfully against her lips. "Honestly?"

"Honestly."

"You won't get upset?" Lisa persisted.

"Of course not," Jessie assured her. "You are my friend. I know you have my best interests at heart."

"Well, I do," Lisa said. "All the same, I'm not sure if you'll care for what I suggest."

Jessie waved the pencil in the air. "Suggest away. I have an open mind on this and really need some feedback."

"All right," Lisa said with a sigh. "The first thing I'd do is think about wardrobe."

Jessie stared at her. "Wardrobe? There isn't any wardrobe, Lisa. These are real people, not actors."

"Did you look at some of them?" Lisa asked. "Jessie, there are some real fashion disasters among those real people. No one is going to want to visit any of these restaurants when they see that the clientele has absolutely no fashion sense. Atmosphere is not just the surroundings of the restaurant but the people surrounding you *in* the restaurant."

"That isn't the point," Jessie said. "Besides, I don't remember seeing anyone who looked too bad."

Lisa was stunned. "You didn't? What about that man in the pink-and-orange Hawaiian shirt and purple shorts?"

Jessie gave her an amused look. "Maybe he's color-blind or related to Screech," she suggested. "Besides, Lisa, lots of tourists wear wild shirts and shorts."

"He was wearing black socks with sandals," Lisa pointed out, sure that her friend hadn't taken in the man's whole ensemble.

"I have a great-uncle who dresses like that," Jessie confessed. "I'll bet a lot of people know some-one who does. Seeing someone like that man in my video will show that the customers are really normal folks."

"Or it could make them lose their appetite," Lisa countered. "I'm just giving you a friendly hint, Jessie. You wanted to know what I'd do? Well, I'd get some attractive people in a tasteful blend of clothing to sit at a table, and I'd concentrate on them, not the restaurant as a whole."

Jessie tossed her notebook aside. "That's stupid, Lisa. It's artificial and doesn't show what Palisades is really like day-to-day."

"I wonder if the Palisades Beautification Committee has seen these people?" Lisa mused aloud. "I'm sure they wouldn't want the Visitors Bureau trying to lure more like them to the area."

"Fashion isn't everything," Jessie said.

Lisa's jaw dropped open.

"Well, it isn't," Jessie insisted. "There are many more important things like clean air, endangered species, and world peace."

"I know that," Lisa said. "But the object of this video is supposed to be to make people outside of Palisades want to visit here. Knowing it's a community with fashion sense would be a plus."

The angle at which Jessie's jaw was clenched told Lisa her friend didn't agree with her.

"Let's just forget that I asked for your help," Jessie suggested as she grabbed her video out of the VCR. "I'll just have to work something out on my own."

"With people like the man in those weird clothes in it, you might as well ask Screech what he thinks," Lisa declared jokingly, relieved that she was off the hook.

Eww. Lisa shuddered. Talk about horror movies. She hadn't seen anything that bad since a date had taken her to watch *Slime Monsters from Planet Zedulon*. Talk about inappropriate costuming!

Still, with more than one entry for the Channel 17 contest among her friends, Lisa was sure that there was one person who was taking advantage of the fact.

And if Zack was taking bets on whether Slater or Jessie would produce the winning video, Lisa wanted to put herself on the side of the victor.

The door had barely closed behind Jessie when Lisa leaped for the phone.

▲   ▼   ▲

Jessie was a block away and still fuming over Lisa's last remark when she suddenly realized just how right Lisa had been.

Oh, not about the need to have better fashions in her video. Designer clothes had nothing in common with organic gardening or vegetarian menus. Lisa was a wonderful friend, but she was very shortsighted when it came to wider issues. At times it seemed as if Lisa's life began and ended at the mall. That wasn't totally true, of course. Lisa was torn between pursuing a career in fashion design or becoming a doctor like both her parents. Jessie had no such problem. Her goal was to attend the best college possible and work toward a law degree. Her mother was able to do a lot of good for the community as a public defender, and Jessie wanted to follow in her footsteps.

But Lisa had been right on the nose in suggesting that Screech would be the perfect person for her to consult about the video. Not only did he have a wardrobe that rivaled that of the man in the Hawaiian shirt, but he was a wiz when it came to editing videos.

Wasting no more time, Jessie turned at the next corner and drove quickly to the Powers home a few blocks away.

Screech's eyes nearly popped out of his head when Jessie waltzed into his room. It was nearly as big as a two-car garage and filled with things that looked like parts of a mad scientist's nightmare. A robot sat in one corner, while on a table a coil of wire twisted toward the ceiling from a series of glass tubes that occasionally glowed and made zapping sounds.

"Jessie!" Screech gulped in surprise. "What are you doing here?"

Jessie slapped her video in his hand. "I need your help, Screech. You're the only person who can help me now."

"Me!"

Jessie nodded solemnly. "You, Screech. Of all our

friends, who, besides me, actually likes to eat vegetables?"

"Me," Screech declared. "I'll eat anything."

"Who, besides me, has ever set foot inside a health food store?"

"Me?" he asked, his voice breaking with a squeaky sound. "I was worried about those wheat germs. I wouldn't want to catch one, you know."

"And," Jessie continued, "who, besides me, is interested in organic farming?"

"Just as a sideline," Screech insisted modestly. "My gerbil is fond of soybean stalks."

"So, who but you would be interested in the same kind of project as I am?" Jessie asked.

Screech scratched his head in thought. "Gee, I don't know, Jessie. Who?"

"You!"

"Me? Wow! What do I have to do?" he demanded.

Jessie tapped the video still resting in his hand. "Fix this, Screech. That's all. Just fix this."

Chapter 10

▲ ▼ ▲ ▼ ▲

After her session with Jessie and phone call to Zack, Lisa found her nerves were tingling so much she couldn't sit still. Zack's news that Kelly was thinking of doing a video had made it impossible to decide which of her friends to cheer for in the contest. And she was still stunned over the realization that Jessie was immune to the soothing qualities found only in gazing upon a correctly appareled community. Jessie had her own style, sometimes a bit careless, but always well put together. As an advocate for improving the environment, Jessie should be concerned about national—even international—fashion sense. Perhaps the psychology of fashion was too subtle to have made an impression on her brainy friend, Lisa mused.

To soothe her own troubled soul, Lisa hurried off to the mall. Even Zack's assurance that he was supervising Slater's climb to the winner's circle hadn't satisfied her need to submerge herself among the soothing fashion bargains available at the shops.

One quick run down each of the mall wings to take a quick look in various store windows and she'd be able to come up with a decent shopping plan, Lisa decided. If she did the spokelike aisles in an orderly fashion, beginning, say, in the northernmost and working clockwise back to it, she could be ready to seriously address any matter, to tackle any problem, no matter how awesome it appeared.

Lisa took a quick turn, headed due north, and ran smack into Kelly.

"Ooooph!" Kelly's breath rushed out in a whoosh of air.

"Whoa! Watch it, honey. I didn't see you!" Lisa cried, grabbing hold of her friend before she fell.

Kelly was wearing her uniform from Yogurt 4-U. It wasn't the most attractive outfit, but on Kelly even the dull uniform had a certain fashion flair.

Lisa breathed easier, her sense of what was right in the world appeased once more.

"I was hoping you'd be here!" Kelly cried happily. "I was headed for Très Charmant to see if you were looking over their new arrivals."

Très Charmant was Lisa's favorite shop in the

mall. "Their new arrivals are in?" Lisa repeated, her eyes glazing a bit in pleasure. "Lead me there!"

Kelly giggled. "Oh, it's so nice to know that at least one of my friends is still the same."

That got Lisa's attention. "Who isn't?" she asked.

"Everyone else! Well, nearly. I don't suppose Screech ever changes."

Lisa rolled her eyes. "It would be a miracle if he did." She linked arms with Kelly and pulled her down the mall in the direction of Très Charmant. "Of course, Jessie's been pretty weird herself lately."

"Tell me about it!" Kelly sighed. "I'm not sure if she's even talking to me anymore. She wanted my help on her video but didn't like anything I suggested."

"Same here," Lisa said. "So, who else is being weird?"

"Slater, I suppose. But he started all this by acting a bit sneaky over the scholarship contest," Kelly said. "Most of all, Zack is not acting at all like himself."

"Zack?" Lisa nearly walked right past Très Charmant, she was so surprised. "What do you mean?"

Kelly took advantage of Lisa's shock to draw her over to a bench. She knew from experience that getting Lisa's full attention inside any shop was impossible.

"He took me to see Mitch's new movie last night," Kelly confessed.

"Zack?" Lisa bleated again. "We are talking about Zack *Morris*?"

"Uh-huh. And he was really sweet about it. He didn't make any stupid cracks, and we didn't go to the Max afterward."

"Didn't go to the Max?"

Kelly giggled again. "You sound like a parrot. I know it's amazing, but . . ."

"Amazing? Girl, it's miraculous!" Lisa insisted. "He actually took my advice!"

Kelly's smile faded. "Zack asked your advice about me?"

Lisa shook her head. "No, not about you in particular, except that it probably was about you in particular! Gosh! I can't believe it."

"What are you talking about?" Kelly demanded.

"About Zack. He said he was taking a survey about the things girls found romantic. I thought he had a new scam going and was going to sell advice to guys who need all the help they can get when it comes to dating," Lisa said. "So, what else happened last night?"

Kelly shrugged. "Not much. We went to the movie. It was really wonderful, Lisa. I cried a lot. Zack gave me his handkerchief. Which reminds me, I've got to get some heavy-duty stain remover to get the mascara out of it before I give it back to him."

Lisa's face went all soft and dreamy. "He gave you his handkerchief to wipe your eyes? What else?"

"Well, he put his arm around me and didn't try to make any of his usual moves when he did."

Lisa's eyes widened in disbelief.

"And when he took me home, he kissed me really tenderly. It was so soft and fleeting, I wasn't really sure he had kissed me," Kelly admitted.

Lisa sighed happily.

"It was wonderfully romantic, but it was weird for Zack. I mean, if there is any boy I know really well, it's Zack Morris," Kelly said.

Lisa grabbed Kelly's hands and squeezed them. "So, do you like the new Zack Morris?"

"Like him?" Kelly grinned at her friend. "Are you kidding? I love him! But it won't last. Nothing ever does between Zack and me. You'd think I'd learn my lesson. Face it, Lisa, if I let him see I'm even tempted to get back together, he'll just start doing all the same old things again."

"Maybe not," Lisa said.

"Don't be silly. The first pretty girl who flutters her lashes at him will have Zack lying to me while he sneaks off with her. It's happened one time after another," Kelly reminded her.

"Maybe he's finally realized what he lost when

you broke up with him," Lisa offered. "It could happen. After all, he did call me for advice, and he did take it."

"I don't know," Kelly murmured. "I've been hurt too many times, Lisa."

"But this is Zack," Lisa insisted. "Face it, girl. Have you ever felt even a smidgen in love with any of the other guys you've dated?"

"A little bit."

"You did for maybe a couple of days," Lisa said. "But you've been more than half in love with Zack for years, haven't you?"

"Well . . ."

"You have," Lisa declared firmly. "You know it and I know it. So I think you should give Zack another chance."

"Well . . ."

Lisa got to her feet and, hands on her hips, stood adamantly before her friend. "Kelly Kathleen Kapowski! Don't you dare let this chance get away from you."

Kelly looked away down the mall a moment before meeting Lisa's eyes. "Okay," she said. "I'll give Zack a chance to prove he really does care about me."

Lisa sighed deeply and sank back on the bench next to Kelly. "I'm so glad you found me and told me. My only advice now is not to let Zack know what you know and just enjoy all the special attention he gives you."

"Absolutely," Kelly agreed with a grin. "But this isn't what I was looking for you to talk about."

Lisa was stunned again. "Then what was it?"

Kelly's smile grew wider. "I'm going to enter the scholarship contest, and I want you to be my consultant on it. You see, I think that people look for a romantic place to visit on their vacation. With the beautiful beaches and pleasant year-round weather, I think Palisades is a very romantic spot. My video will show just that. But it needs more than just pretty backgrounds to be convincing. It also needs gorgeous people in fantastic clothes."

"Clothes?" Lisa repeated. "Did you say clothes?"

"I don't know anyone who is more up on the latest fashions," Kelly said, "or who knows lots of gorgeous-looking guys we could ask to be in the video."

Mentally, Lisa was already making a list and picking out the perfect wardrobe for each.

"And, of course, there is one other thing I need you to help me with," Kelly added.

"Name it," Lisa declared. "What is mine, girl, is yours." After all, she added silently to herself, what better way to make sure she was on the victor's side than to be part of the team. Jessie's video was hopelessly dull, and Slater's sounded hopelessly macho. But Kelly's idea . . . ah, now there was a winner in the making.

"I've got some great ideas," Kelly said, "but I

can't put them all together without this one thing. Do you think your parents would let me borrow their video camera?"

"No problem," Lisa assured her. "No problem at all."

▲   ▼   ▲

Zack swung through the open window of Slater's bedroom, a contented smile on his face. "It's in the bag, pal," he announced. "Jessie hasn't got a chance. Her subject is strictly Dull City."

"Yeah," Slater mumbled from where he was stretched out on his bed. There were brochures spilling off the end of the bedspread. "Great."

He didn't sound like anything was great.

Zack frowned at his buddy. "I don't think I could stand it if you showed any more enthusiasm. The shouts of joy are so deafening already."

Slater shrugged. "Sorry, preppie. It's just hard to get excited about winning anymore."

Zack nodded and dropped down in a chair, his legs stretched out before him. "Too sure a deal, huh? Well, what can I say? When you're good, you're good."

"It isn't that," Slater said. "It's my dad. He's the one who's really excited about the contest."

"Yeah? Hey, that's great! Oh, I get it. We know what Jessie's working on, but there might be some other contenders out there to worry about. It proba-bly would be a good idea to sniff out the rest of the competition, hmm?" Zack slumped lower in his chair. "I'll get Screech right on it. With his computer hacker abilities and my brains, we'll find out who has entered and then . . ."

"It isn't that," Slater said again. "Like I said, it's my dad. He came up with these." Slater tossed one of the brochures over to where Zack sat.

Zack caught it one-handed and flipped through it. "Houndslow Heath U?"

"Dad wants me to go there so he can request reassignment in England."

"And?" Zack asked, still not understanding what the problem was.

"And I don't want to go," Slater said. "But I can't tell him that. He'd never understand. He loves traveling to foreign places. We've been in California long enough to make him anxious to move on again."

"You mean he wants to leave California for good?" Zack demanded, clearly stunned that anyone would choose to do so.

"Relax, preppie," Slater suggested. "It's me he wants to move, not you."

"Can't you just tell your dad you want to stay here for school?"

"Yeah, sure. Could you tell your dad something like that if you knew he had his heart set on you doing something else?" Slater asked.

Zack pondered the question. "Actually," he said, "it's my mother who wants me to go to Princeton, not my dad. But I see your dilemma. What are you going to do?"

Slater sighed deeply, then sat up straight. "I think I'll fill out this application to Houndslow Heath and hope they turn me down," he said.

"Any chance that will happen?" Zack asked.

"Not a chance," Slater admitted sadly. "Not a single chance."

Chapter 11

▲ ▼ ▲ ▼ ▲

Sunday evening Kelly shot around the front room of the Kapowski home as if jet-propelled. She ran a finger along the mantle checking for dust, then rearranged the frames of all the family photographs making sure that pictures she hated were well hidden. She fluffed every throw pillow in sight.

Mrs. Kapowski and Lisa stood in the hall and shook their heads in wonder.

"I've never seen such diligence in straightening up before," Kelly's mother said. There was a smile in her voice and in her eyes.

"If I'd known she was going to freak like this, I never would have suggested asking Mitch to drop by this evening to give us his professional opinion," Lisa said.

Kelly stopped in the middle of the room and frowned at her surroundings. "There's something wrong with this place," she declared. "I just can't put my finger on what the problem is."

"Relax," Lisa urged. "The place looks like something in a decorating magazine."

"Which is what makes it look strange, sweetheart," Mrs. Kapowski explained. "It's the first time since your oldest brother was born that there hasn't been a toy or two lying in the middle of the floor."

Kelly chewed her lip in indecision. "You really think that's why it looks weird?"

Mrs. Kapowski glided into the room and gave Kelly a bracing hug. "I know it is." She surveyed the room, a satisfied grin curving her lips. "In fact, it looks so good, I'm tempted to ask Mr. Tobias to drop by on a regular basis so you are inspired to clean this well more often."

"Don't joke, Mom," Kelly pleaded. "This is really important. It's for scholarship money. Lisa and I worked like mad filming since yesterday afternoon. And Mitch is doing us a big favor by watching our video and giving us his opinion."

"Yes, I know," Mrs. Kapowski said. "It's nice to see success hasn't spoiled him and he's still a good friend to you."

Kelly hugged her mother back. "Thanks, Mom. Now, are you sure Erin or Billy or Nicki won't be running in while Mitch is here? Oh, or worse! Kirby,

Kerry, or Kyle won't be coming home unexpectedly, will they?"

Mrs. Kapowski not only assured Kelly her siblings would not interrupt, she went on to list in detail where the three younger children and the three older boys were, to soothe Kelly's anxiety. When she finished, Kelly looked a bit calmer.

Or she did until she caught sight of herself in the mirror that hung over the mantle. "Oh! Look at my hair! Lisa, are you sure this outfit is right? You don't think this pink has too much red in it? And what about my lipstick? Too much bronze in it?"

The sound of a car outside the house drew Lisa to the window. "It's fine. You look great. The pink is perfect and your lipstick matches it. And besides, it's too late to change. Mitch is here," she announced, as she peeked through the venetian blinds at the bright yellow convertible sports car now parked out front.

Kelly nearly started hyperventilating. While Mrs. Kapowski went to answer the door, Lisa rubbed Kelly's shoulders.

"Relax," she ordered. "It's only Mitch."

"Who is a big movie star," Kelly said.

"Who was a taxi driver," Lisa countered. "Who you talked to on the phone very recently."

"Who will probably hate our video," Kelly declared with a gulp. "Oh, Lisa! What if he does hate it?"

Lisa rubbed her friend's shoulders harder. "Don't even think about it," she instructed.

Out in the hall they could hear Mrs. Kapowski greeting the actor.

"Okay now?" Lisa asked, giving Kelly a last shake.

Kelly took a deep breath. "I hope so."

She had donned a brilliant smile by the time Mitch followed her mother into the room.

Despite his recent rise to fame, Mitch didn't look much different than he had when he'd been driving a cab. His hair was still black and very curly, his eyes were still an electric blue, and more importantly, his grin was still the crooked, infectious one that had charmed Kelly the first time she saw him.

"Hi!" he greeted. "How's my favorite acting student?"

Kelly just managed to hold back a melting sigh. He was so handsome. No wonder women were flocking to see his movies.

"Hi! Oh, I'm fine. You remember my friend Lisa, don't you?"

"I never forget a beautiful woman," he insisted, and winked at Lisa.

Lisa dropped down in a chair, her eyes a bit dazed, and her expression all dreamy.

So much for her pep talk about how it was *just Mitch*, Kelly thought ruefully.

"It was really sweet of you to take time out for this, Mitch," Kelly said.

"After you gave me such a glowing report on the

new movie? It's the least I could do, Kelly." When he flashed his now famous grin again, Kelly was pretty sure she heard her mother give a dreamy-sounding sigh.

"Well, where is it?" Mitch asked. "I'm anxious to see what you've put together." He took a seat on the sofa directly in front of the family television.

Since Mrs. Kapowski took the living-room chair across from Lisa, Kelly was left with no place else to sit other than next to him. She picked up the remote control and hit the play button.

"It will probably look pretty amateurish to you, Mitch, but—"

"Shh," he admonished. "No buttering up the reviewer. Besides, everyone has to start somewhere."

Kelly buttoned her lip as the TV screen brightened to show a pure blue sky before dipping to a deeper blue ocean. A lone surfer glided on a white-capped wave. Soft romantic music accompanied the film with Kelly's voice joining it as she read love poetry over the muted roar of the surf.

Anyone around Bayside would have recognized the surfer as Cal Everhart, one of Lisa's former boyfriends, but all anyone else would see was a tall, muscular, tanned, blond, and incredibly handsome young man. He glided his board inland, the sun behind him like a theatrical backlight, and ran lightly through the shallows to meet a girl with long red hair. Lisa had hated asking Veronica Courtland to play opposite Cal, but her sense of color had insisted

Veronica's hair would photograph well next to Cal's. Veronica wore a softly draped sundress that enhanced her own deep tan.

Kelly glanced at Mitch. He was smiling. *Smiling!* That was good. She relaxed a bit and turned her attention back to the video.

Cal dropped his arm around Veronica's shoulders as the couple strolled off down the beach into the setting sun. Then the scene shifted to a candlelit restaurant and another couple. Jeremy Frears, a hurdler on the track team, had been paired with Phyllis Ptowski, a pretty blond. On the video, Jeremy looked like a boy ready to sink into Phyllis's big brown eyes. They held hands and ignored the full-course meal spread out on the table before them. Jeremy was in a tuxedo; Phyllis was dazzling in a strapless gown decorated with midnight blue sequins.

Mitch made a noise that sounded like he was strangling or trying to disguise a cough. He was so sweet, Kelly thought. He didn't want to miss any of the love poem being read, this time over the sound of violins and the slight clatter of china.

Another scene shift showed Dee Dee Horwitzer with her arms around Denny Vane as they roared down the Pacific Coast Highway on his motorcycle. Denny wore his usual leather (Lisa hadn't been able to convince him to wear anything else), and Dee Dee looked dramatically windblown in designer jeans, tube top, and three-inch-high red heels.

Mitch leaned forward, his hands on the knees of his jeans. His smile stretched nearly ear-to-ear! Kelly could barely control her excitement. He liked it!

Back on the screen, Jean-Marie Howell was snuggling with Tony Annuncio in the front seat of a convertible that was parked to give a breathtaking view of Palisades at night. Although Lisa had sweated over the wardrobe for this scene, in the dark it was impossible to see what wonders she had found for them to wear.

Kelly read another poem, and harp music filled the air.

The scene faded to black only to be replaced by a carefully hand-lettered poster that read: PALISADES— WHERE ROMANCE IS ALWAYS IN THE AIR.

The Kapowski living room was silent when the tape ran out.

Mitch took a handkerchief from his back pocket, wiped his eyes, and made a few more of those half strangled sounds. He must have allergies, Kelly decided.

Mrs. Kapowski burst into applause and hastily asked if anyone would like a snack. Then she vanished into the back of the house, leaving Kelly and Lisa both poised and waiting for Mitch's first words.

Mitch stuffed his handkerchief away and ran a hand back through his curly dark hair. He cleared his voice. "Bravo," he murmured, beaming happily at both Lisa and Kelly.

The girls looked at each other. Bravo? He should have shouted it, shouldn't he? At least he should if he thought the video was good.

And if it wasn't?

Eww.

"You girls have filmed a wonderful satire. I don't think you missed picking up a single scene that hasn't been used in a romantic context in the movie world," Mitch continued, and wiped his eyes again with his fingers.

Those were tears of laughter, not allergies, Kelly realized.

"In fact," Mitch said enthusiastically, "I think the perfume manufacturers of the world would love to get their hands on this. It's so camp. So hokey. So fantastically—"

Mitch broke off and looked from Kelly to Lisa. "Uh-oh. Blew that one, didn't I?" he asked. "It wasn't supposed to be funny, was it?"

"No," Kelly agreed in a small voice. "It was supposed to make people want to come to Palisades on vacation."

"It might do that," Mitch said.

Kelly and Lisa exchanged a look.

"It might not," Lisa said.

Mrs. Kapowski dashed back into the room with a tray in her hands. "Lemonade anyone?"

Kelly and Lisa slumped in their seats. Mitch jumped to his feet. "I hate to drink and run," he told

Kelly's mother as he gulped down lemonade, "but I think I hear my agent calling me."

Mrs. Kapowski glanced at Kelly's and Lisa's glum faces. "I sure wish he were calling me, too," she said.

Chapter 12

▲ ▼ ▲ ▼ ▲

Zack had just finished watching Slater's video for perhaps the zillionth time that evening when his cellular phone rang. Pleased to have an excuse to stop viewing the short film, he palmed the phone a millisecond after the first ring. Across the room, Slater frowned at him, as if he considered answering the phone an infringement on his duties as coproducer.

Zack didn't care. He was pretty sure he'd reached the bounds of friendship and gone far beyond it in enduring Slater's obsession with the contest. If Slater didn't head overseas to attend school in England, Zack thought maybe *he* would, just to get away from Slater.

At the moment, the phone was his escape.

"Morris is the name, scamming's the game," he announced into the receiver.

"Don't I know it," Kelly's sweet voice said.

Zack sat up straighter. "Kelly!" he croaked in surprise.

Slater's eyebrows rose in surprise as well. Although once Kelly had frequently called just to talk, Zack couldn't remember her doing it much since they'd broken up.

"I'm not disturbing you, am I?" Kelly asked.

"No way."

"Wellll," Kelly said, drawing out the word as if she was unsure of herself or of his reaction to her call. "I was just wondering if you'd like to go to a movie. The newspaper has an ad for *Martial Arts Justice: The Final Kick*. It's the sequel to your favorite movie."

Zack was flabbergasted! Maybe he'd been right to take Lisa's advice about romance. He'd taken Kelly to see something she wanted to see, and now she was offering to go to a movie he wanted to see. This doing what the other person wanted must work both ways.

All right!

"If you're free," Kelly continued, "and can pick me up, I'll treat you to it."

"I'll be there in five minutes," Zack promised, and leaped to his feet. "You're on your own, buddy," he told Slater.

"Great. At least you aren't asking me to shell out any cash tonight. That has to be a plus," Slater said, and leaned over to turn off the television. "Besides, I don't think there's anything else I can do to this. Part of me wants to win the contest, but part of me doesn't want to anymore. Either way, I don't think I have a problem. This film isn't going to make it. It's only three minutes long, and the rules state that the video has to be exactly five minutes. The deadline is Monday, you know. Tomorrow."

Zack was already halfway through the window. "Don't worry," he shouted back. "I'll think of something to help you."

"Yeah, sure," Slater mumbled. "Don't strain your brain for me, preppie. I'll survive. Somehow," he added under his breath.

Zack didn't hear. He was already gunning the engine of his Mustang.

▲   ▼   ▲

Jessie sat in the Powers family room and watched as the frames flickered by on the television screen. She had hit the timer of the stopwatch Screech had handed her when the film began. Now she hit it again as the final scene finished.

"Screech! You are a genius!" she shouted. "This is amazing! It's exactly five minutes long. Not four minutes and fifty-nine seconds, not five minutes and one second, but exactly five minutes on the nose."

Screech polished his fingernails against his shirt front. "Nothing that any genius couldn't handle," he murmured modestly.

"How did you do it?" Jessie demanded. "I know

you had to cut things, but I didn't feel that anything was missing."

"That's because I didn't cut anything. I speeded up the film instead."

"Well, I did think that some of those waiters were moving awfully quick," Jessie admitted. "But I just thought they were giving fast service."

"Which is a good selling point," Screech noted.

"And the customers look so animated and hungry since they are moving more quickly."

"Also a good selling point," Screech said. "Now all we have to do is cut a new voice-over with you telling about the artichokes and the restaurants, I'll dub the whole thing together, and it will be finished."

"That's it?" Jessie jumped to her feet and hugged Screech quickly. "You're wonderful!" she declared.

Screech blushed about six different shades of pink.

"When will you have it ready?" Jessie asked.

Screech pondered a moment. His head bobbed back and forth, he counted a bit on his fingers, licked one finger and held it up to check wind direction, then looked at his watch. "Not long," he announced.

Jessie grabbed her purse. "Then I won't keep you." She handed him a cassette with the audio track she'd already done. "Here you are. I can't wait to see the final product. In fact, I'll treat you to as many Max-imum burgers as you can eat by way of thanking you for all your work."

Screech's eyes grew large. "Now that's a thank you I can sink my teeth into!" he said. "Shall we rendezvous at the Max in three hours?"

"You got it," Jessie said, and sailed out of the room.

▲ ▼ ▲

Kelly walked along the beach, her sandals in one hand. The surf washed up to swirl around her ankles and those of Zack as he strolled along next to her. Their linked hands swung companionably back and forth.

"So it looks like I'm not going to enter the scholarship contest after all," Kelly said. "Lisa and I decided to give our film a burial at sea, except, of course, that would be littering, so we just hid it far back in the TV cabinet."

She walked on a few steps before asking. "How's Slater doing?"

"Terrible," Zack confessed. "He lost his edge when his dad got enthusiastic about the project."

"But that's great," Kelly insisted. "Slater is dying to have his father interested in what he's doing."

"*Was* dying to," Zack corrected. "Since Major Slater got excited about this school in England and intends to move the whole family there, Slater's looked more like he was trampled by the Valley High football team. The only time he even looks a little like his old self is when his dad is around, and then he's just acting." Zack paused and kicked at a bit of surf foam. "Slater's miserable, Kel. But he doesn't want to hurt his dad's feelings."

"Gosh, I wish there was something we could do to help him," Kelly said. "Is his video really bad?"

"No, it's just too short."

"Well, if my tape wasn't so awful, I'd let him use it," she offered. "Though that won't keep his dad from sending him to London."

Zack nodded. "Yeah, the only way Slater will be able to stay in California is if his application is turned down by Houndslow. Since the major is calling in favors to make sure that doesn't happen, Slater doesn't have much of a chance. Unless . . ." His voice trailed off.

Zack stopped walking. With her hand in his, Kelly was jerked to a sudden halt. She nearly dropped her sandals in the water.

"Unless a recruiter from Houndslow Heath arrived here in Palisades and turned Slater's application down immediately," Zack mused.

Kelly studied him closely. "I know that look," she declared. "You've got an idea that will get Slater out of this spot, don't you?"

An anxious look crossed Zack's face. Kelly hated most of his scams. The chance to patch things up with her was beckoning him; this was not the time to pull a fast one. Even if it would help Slater.

"Who? Me? No way," Zack insisted. "I've gotten in enough trouble pulling scams. I've learned my lesson. I'm never going to do it again. Honest."

Kelly smiled softly. "It's okay, Zack. If you know a way to help Slater, I think you should do it. And if I can, I'll help you."

Since she squeezed his hand in encouragement, Zack decided to take a chance.

"Okay. I have to make one quick phone call; then we head for the Max," he said.

Kelly let go of his hand and skipped a few steps up the beach and out of the surf. "You always think better after a burger," she agreed. "Let's find a pay phone, and I'll start calling the gang to meet us there. And Zack?"

His mind whirling as the plan formed, Zack was a bit distracted. "Hmm?"

Kelly slid her arms around his neck and went up on her toes as she kissed him quickly.

A pleased smile curled the corners of Zack's mouth. "What was that for?"

"It was a carrot," Kelly said. "Pull this off, and there just might be more of those for you."

Zack dropped his arm around her shoulders and led Kelly back to where he'd parked his car. "Now that's a goal worth working toward," he declared. "Even better than a burger at the Max."

Kelly giggled as she wrapped her arm around his waist. Together they hurried up the beach.

Behind them the sun blazed in gold and red flames as it sank below the horizon. The effect was

like a theatrical backlight. Kelly didn't notice. And
Mitch Tobias wasn't there to see just how romantic
the beach in Palisades could be.

Chapter 13

▲ ▼ ▲ ▼ ▲

When Clorinda Winter arrived, the whole gang, with the exception of Screech, was already seated in their regular booth at the Max.

Zack was a bit nervous as he introduced the pretty English girl to everyone. Especially when it was Kelly's turn. He only breathed easier when Kelly accepted his explanation about meeting Clorinda while they were both in detention.

Clorinda sipped on a chocolate shake and listened quietly as Zack outlined both Slater's problem and the scam he'd come up with to eliminate it.

"Oooh! That's quite a naughty bit of scheming," Clorinda approved. "But what's in it for me?"

"My undying gratitude," Slater said.

Jessie frowned when Clorinda gave him a flirtatious grin.

"I will personally escort you through the mall and introduce you to all the best stores," Lisa offered.

"If you want to be on the cheerleading squad, I'll be glad to coach you in all the cheers for tryouts," Kelly said.

Jessie glanced once from Clorinda to Slater, then sighed. "And if you need help with any kind of homework, I'll be your tutor," she said.

Zack grinned. "See? You can pretty well name your price, Clorinda."

"When?"

"When you're ready," he assured her. "But we need you to make the phone call now. Will you do it?"

"Not worried my services might cost the earth?" Clorinda asked. She looked at each of the gang as if gauging their pockets before she turned to flutter her eyelashes at Zack.

Beneath the tabletop, he took a firm grip on Kelly's hand. "If you pull it off, the price will be worth it."

Zack glanced quickly over at Slater. He himself couldn't chance flirting with Clorinda. Not when he was so close to winning Kelly back. But Slater wasn't going with anyone. If he'd just give Clorinda a dose of those twin dimples, she'd be ready to eat out of Slater's hand. Zack had seen it happen before as girls at Bayside nearly fainted when Slater grinned their way.

Of course, now that he really needed Slater to lay on the charm, his muscle-bound friend's fountain seemed to have dried up.

"I'll bet we could even come up with a good-looking escort to take you to the Surf's Up Beach Party this weekend," Zack said, his eyes all the while locked on Slater's unresponsive form. "Is it a deal?"

Clorinda tossed her red hair back from her face. "It's a deal!" she announced. "Where's the phone?"

Zack picked up his cellular phone and punched in the number for the Slater household, then passed the phone to Clorinda.

While it rang, Kelly squeezed Zack's hand and smiled up into his face. Boy, had he missed those looks, Zack thought. And, boy, was he ever going to have to watch his every step to make sure he never missed them again!

"Mr. Slater?" Clorinda asked when the call was answered. "Oh, I am sorry. *Major* Slater."

Zack barely recognized Clorinda's voice. Her usual casual chirping had been replaced with a very stilted tone that made it sound as if she were speaking through her nose. She sounded like butlers did in old movies.

"This is Aphenia Waldencottle of the Houndslow Heath University School of Broadcasting in London," Clorinda said. "The admissions office tells me that you and your son are interested in our fine institution. Since I was touring this area on a recruitment mission, I gave a pop round to this Bayside High School last week and had a look at your son's records."

She paused a moment while Major Slater said something. "Oh, yes. We at Houndslow Heath are always pleased when Americans consider joining our excellent program. And I'm pleased to tell you I was very impressed with Albert's academic progress."

Slater flinched at the sound of his given name.

"Oh, he goes by his initials?" Clorinda said into the phone. "How very American, my dear major. And how sad. Albert is such a lovely name."

Slater cringed.

"The late Queen Victoria did so adore her own Albert," Clorinda continued. "But it is of your Albert that we speak, dear sir. You see, while he has an impressive record, I'm afraid it still falls a bit shy of what we are forced to require for broadcast studies at Houndslow Heath."

A slight smile surfaced on Slater's previously sad face.

"Yes, yes, I quite understand that you may have heard differently from various people," Clorinda said, "but the truth of the matter is that we have so many applicants from around the world that we are able to accept only a handful. Yes, yes, we members of the faculty and staff are quite in sympathy with you there, Major. But, alas, there are insufficient funds to expand our facilities to meet the needs of these well-deserving applicants. I thought it only right to give you the news straightaway so that Albert—oh, yes, I am so sorry—so that A. C. can devote his energies to discovering a worthy school elsewhere. Perhaps here in your own sunny California?"

A moment later, Clorinda handed Zack's phone back to him.

Slater sighed in relief. "You are indeed a girl without price," he said.

Clorinda put her elbows on the table and dropped her chin in her upturned hands. "Oh, I wouldn't say that, luv. I've a price in mind."

"The Surf's Up party," Slater said. "I would be honored to take you, Clorinda."

"I'd be honored to go," she said. "But that's rather paltry payment for my services, wouldn't you say?" She turned wide eyes on Zack.

He suddenly felt as if the neck of his T-shirt had shrunk and was choking him.

"You're a right handsome chap and all, Albert," Clorinda soothed. She patted Slater's hand. "And I'm sure I'll be a regular Cinderella with you giving me your full attention at the party Saturday. But let's face it, you couldn't have pulled this little scam without me, could you?"

"Wellll," Zack began.

"You couldn't," Clorinda said. "Albert's papa would have recognized any of your voices, wouldn't he?"

Zack swallowed loudly.

"Probably," Kelly admitted.

"And my accent was far more authentic," Clorinda continued. "More believable."

"True," Lisa said.

"And the situation was pretty desperate, wasn't it?" Clorinda continued.

"Was it ever," Slater murmured.

Zack could see the price Clorinda planned on asking skyrocketing out of control.

"One paltry party for all that?" Clorinda purred. "For shame. I would expect at least two frivolous evenings as payment for my performance."

"So would I," Jessie announced, suddenly jumping in on Clorinda's side. "And the second one should be a nice dinner, a movie, and a moonlit drive along the beach."

Clorinda grinned widely at her. "Oh, I do like that idea."

Slater cleared his throat and glared across the table at Zack. Zack could almost hear his friend slowly counting the little bit of cash that was left in his wallet after Zack had grazed through it.

"I don't know if I can—" Slater said, but Clorinda cut him off quickly.

"I wouldn't put you to the trouble two days in a row, dearie," she insisted. "But I'm sure someone else could handle this little detail."

She gave Zack a sublime smile. "And I think you're just the chap to handle it," she purred.

Zack felt Kelly's hand steal from his grasp. Felt the cold chill of rejection once more.

"What an excellent idea, Clorinda," Kelly announced. "Don't you agree, Lisa? Jessie? Slater?"

With his friends all staring at him in suspicion and nodding their agreement, Zack wished he could sink lower in his seat. They thought he'd pulled a double scam! He could read it in their eyes. He had found a way to save Slater, but they thought he had also finagled a way to date Clorinda without looking as if he were chasing her!

"Zack?" Clorinda asked.

Zack sighed deeply. "I agree. You deserve dinner and a movie."

"Make it this Sunday," she said. "And, Zack, don't forget to include that romantic trip to the beach. I'd hate to think you were a slacker."

▲   ▼   ▲

The gang waited only until Clorinda left before turning on him.

"Slick, preppie," Slater said. "Really slick."

Zack ran a hand back through his blond hair. "I didn't know she would insist that we both date her," he pleaded. "If I had, do you think I would—"

"Yes," Jessie said. "We know it."

"It's a good thing Screech wasn't here," Kelly commented. "She probably would have wanted to have a date with him, too."

"Eww." Lisa shivered. "No one could be that

desperate, even if they are new at Bayside."

"Speaking of Screech," Jessie murmured, "he was supposed to be here half an hour ago. Anyone know what happened to him?"

Zack shrugged.

"Maybe you gave him too big a chore with your video," Kelly suggested.

Zack was surprised to hear disapproval in Kelly's voice. She and Jessie had been friends since elementary school. Now they looked at each other like two cats about to fight. He could almost see their backs arching and their brightly painted nails turning into claws.

"Yeah," Lisa said. "What did you do? Ask him to do a sound track of organically approved music?"

Slater and Zack exchanged puzzled looks. Lisa was mad at Jessie, too? This was a first! Apparently working on a video for scholarship money had turned friends into enemies.

At least that hadn't happened to him and Slater, Zack mused.

Slater's glare became anything but friendly.

No, it wasn't the video that turned Slater into an enemy. It was Clorinda.

Zack sighed loudly. When would he ever learn?

"Here's Screech," Kelly announced as the front door of the Max crashed open and Screech tumbled into the room.

Screech always looked a bit wild, but he looked

even more so right then. His hair stood up on end, one of his mauve-and-chartreuse sneakers was untied, and he'd buttoned his shirt crooked so it was two buttons out of sync.

"Jessie!" Screech gasped, sliding to a stop at the table. "Something terrible has happened!"

"Not to my video!" she moaned.

Screech looked impressed. "Yes. How did you know?" He regarded her suspiciously. "Did you read my mind?"

"What happened?" Jessie demanded. "Couldn't you get the audio to mix with the video?"

Screech sank down into the chair Clorinda had vacated. "Oh no. That was no problem. I dubbed off a new copy so the editing wasn't apparent."

Jessie wilted in her seat. "Oh, good."

"Well, not so good," Screech admitted reluctantly. "You see, I rewound the new copy and left it in the VCR while I erased the original tapes. I was being frugal, you see, and recycling them for future use."

"And then what happened?"

"I got hungry and went to the kitchen to grab a snack. The trouble is, while I was gone, my parents decided to tape a show about aardvarks, and . . . well . . ."

"Don't tell me," Jessie insisted. "They taped over my video, didn't they?"

"You told me not to tell you," Screech reminded her.

"Didn't you have it labeled?"

"Not yet," he said. "I'm sorry, Jessie. I know how much entering this contest meant to you. We can shoot it again."

Slater shook his head sadly. "I'm afraid not, Screech. The deadline is tomorrow. Looks like none of us will be entering."

"Yeah," Lisa said. "After all the work we did, too."

Jessie collapsed back in the booth. "You mean you didn't finish yours, Kelly?"

"Oh, Lisa and I finished it, all right," Kelly said with a groan. "We even had Mitch Tobias over to watch it. He thought it was hilarious."

"That's good," Zack insisted.

"No, it isn't," Lisa said.

"What went wrong with yours, Slater?" Jessie asked. "You started long before any of us."

"Yep. And it's still two minutes short," Slater said.

Jessie sank lower in her seat. "Mine was too long."

"Too bad you don't have any footage left," Zack said. "You could add some to Slater's and—"

Kelly jumped in her seat and gave Zack a quick hug. He was so astounded, his mouth dropped open.

"But Lisa and I have footage you could use!" Kelly told Slater. "If Screech can edit it all together so that it seems to make sense, you can still enter the contest. Maybe even win!"

"You're serious?" Slater demanded.

"Absolutely!" Kelly said.

"Then what are we doing sitting here?" he asked. "Let's go."

Chapter 14

▲ ▼ ▲ ▼ ▲

Saturday afternoon the grandstand that had been set up temporarily for the Surf's Up Beach Party was full by the time the news team from KPSD-TV—Channel 17—and the Visitors Bureau were to announce the winner of the video contest.

Zack and the rest of the gang all took seats near the front, with Slater on the aisle so that he could get to the stage to accept the grand prize.

They were surprised that Clorinda wasn't with him, but she'd decided to skip the daytime activities and avoid major sunburn to her fair skin. She'd join them later in the evening, Slater said, his expression resigned to the fact.

There were a lot of other high school seniors in the crowd, and a good number of parents and family members, all eager to share in their contestant's good fortune.

When a heavy hand fell on Zack's shoulder, he had the uncanny feeling of déjà vu. He wasn't surprised when he turned in his seat to confront Mr. Belding.

"Morris," the principal greeted with one of his sickly smiles—the kind Zack recognized as meaning he was in big trouble.

A few seats away, Slater felt a hand fall on his shoulder as well. "Dad!" he gulped. "I didn't think you could make it here today."

"I've just had a very interesting conversation with Mr. Belding," Major Slater said.

"Really? Great!" Slater declared. He didn't sound as if it was very great, though.

"Do you remember when I told you I got a call from a recruiter from Houndslow Heath University last Sunday night?" the major asked.

"Uh, yeah."

"Well, the more I thought about it, the more I was sure something could be done about your admittance application there. The least they could do is let you be on a waiting list. Don't you agree?"

Slater cut a desperate look at Zack, but Zack was trying to be invisible under Mr. Belding's gaze.

"Your father gave me a call yesterday afternoon," Mr. Belding said, "and asked if I knew how to get in touch with a Ms. Waldencottle, whom he believed had been visiting Bayside recently."

Kelly, Lisa, Jessie, and Screech swung their heads back to face Major Slater.

"Imagine my astonishment when Mr. Belding was unaware that there was a Ms. Waldencottle at his school, much less that she had been given free rein in the students' files," the major said.

"We don't allow that," Mr. Belding explained.

The gang turned to look at him.

"And I'm pretty sure that I would have remembered someone with a name like Aphenia Waldencottle. Wouldn't you, Morris?" the principal asked.

Zack swallowed loudly.

"The only person I've met recently who is English is an exchange student named Clorinda Winter," Mr. Belding explained. "So, naturally, I called her into my office for a nice friendly talk."

"A friendly talk?" Zack croaked. "That's very nice, sir. I'm sure it made her feel right at home in a strange land."

"Oh, it made her feel at home, all right," Mr. Belding agreed. "And as a result, I'm going to keep my eye on Clorinda the next few weeks."

Zack shook his head as if he couldn't understand how any student could fall so low as to merit such a punishment.

"Of course, she won't be alone, Morris," Mr. Belding said. "If you get my drift."

Zack swallowed again. "I, er, get your drift," he said.

"Good, good." Mr. Belding patted Zack's shoulder.

Major Slater shook his head sadly. "Why didn't you tell me you didn't want to attend Houndslow Heath, A. C.?"

Slater hung his head. "I couldn't, Dad. You were so excited about it and you wanted reassignment in England so much, I didn't want to disappoint you."

"It wasn't my future we were dealing with, though, son," the major said. "It was yours. And I think you should have a say in what you want to do. Of course, I'll be the first one to admit I'm not looking forward to the time you'll be out on your own. Your mother and I will miss you, A. C. Can you blame us for wanting to be near you when you head off to college?"

"No, it's just that . . ."

"Just what?" Major Slater prompted when Slater didn't finish his statement.

Slater looked up and met his father's eyes. "I don't want to leave here, Dad," he said. "I have friends here. I have a life here. If you and Mom want to be where I am after I graduate from Bayside, then you won't be requesting reassignment. Not anywhere else stateside or anywhere else in the world. I do want to be a broadcaster, but I want to learn to be one here in California."

The major settled his hand on Slater's shoulder once more, but this time in a gesture of pride and affection. "Then this is where I want to be, too, son," he said. "Now, make room for your old man, why don't you? I'd like to be right up front, leading the applause when you win this scholarship money."

It wasn't long before Clark Dieter, the head anchorperson for Channel 17, moved to the microphone and asked everyone to be seated so they could begin.

"We've got a lot of great activities and entertainment planned today, but first we want to thank all the students who participated in the video scholarship contest. It was a difficult decision to choose the winner from all the fine videos that were entered," he told the crowd. "The committee and I spent many long hours this week viewing and reviewing each film before deciding on two finalists."

The gang all exchanged hopeful glances. Zack gave Slater the thumbs-up sign. The girls all crossed their fingers for luck as did Screech, who also screwed his eyes shut and twisted his legs until they resembled a pretzel.

"Of course there can be only one winner. We have only one scholarship check," Clark Dieter said. "So what we've come up with is a sort of secondary prize. It may not be worth nearly as much, but it honors a worthy effort. Now, may I have the envelope please?"

A woman from the Visitors Bureau bounced to her feet and presented him with a cream-colored envelope. The gang waited, holding their breath, while the newsman took his time opening it.

"And the scholarship check goes to Ms. Victoria Flauntmount of Valley High School," he announced. "Ms. Flauntmount's video will be used by the Visitors Bureau in their ongoing efforts to lure more tourists to our fair city. In five short minutes she managed to highlight all the things in Palisades that would draw families to our area."

Jessie leaned from her seat and reached for Slater's hand. "Oh, Slater, I'm so sorry you didn't win."

"Families?" Lisa echoed. "Why didn't any of us think of that?"

"I should have," Kelly said. "Heck, that's the only way my parents ever plan a vacation. They look at everything a place has to offer to entertain us kids."

Screech shook his head as if truly disgusted. "Well, there's one thing for sure, Slater," he said. "Victoria's video wasn't as technically clean as yours was."

"Or as packed full of great-looking guys," Kelly added.

"Or gorgeous girls, pal," Zack reminded. "Heck,

you and I scouted out the cream of Palisades."

Kelly, Lisa, and Jessie stared at him.

"Oh, present company excepted," Zack hastened to add. "We wouldn't want to exploit our best friends, after all. Right?"

"Right, preppie," Slater agreed.

Clark Dieter tapped on the microphone to regain everyone's attention. "Our runner-up video must be honored for its originality. Excessive originality," he said with a grin. "In fact, none of us on the committee had ever seen quite so many young people enjoying life in Palisades before we viewed this film. We found it refreshing to learn our local seniors are making the most of the wonderful sights and places that our town has to offer. And for allowing us that glimpse we are honoring A. C. Slater of Bayside High School with . . ."

Major Slater jumped to his feet and led the yells of delight. Mr. Belding pounded Slater on the back proudly. Jessie hugged Slater fiercely, while Kelly kissed his cheek and Lisa tossed hastily shredded confetti over his head. Screech pumped Slater's hand. But when Zack pushed through the crowd to congratulate his friend, the two boys stared at each other in silence a moment before exchanging a self-conscious bear hug.

"What did you win?" Lisa asked excitedly.

"Better get up there and find out," the major urged.

As he climbed up on the small stage, Slater's smile stretched from ear-to-ear, and his dimples were deep enough to cause a couple of girls in the audience to swoon.

Clark Dieter shook Slater's hand and made sure that the photographers from the newspaper took a picture of the event. Then he handed Slater a huge box. "Just a little something for you and your friends to enjoy," the newsman said.

It wasn't until he got back to his seat and the gang waited breathlessly while he ripped the box open that Slater figured out what the anchorman had meant.

"Wow!" Screech declared with an awestruck sigh when Slater leaned over his prize and then straightened, wearing a pair of comic eyeglasses, a giant red nose, a drooping mustache, and buck teeth. "That's a much better prize than any old scholarship check."

"It sure is," Slater agreed. "Because this is one prize I can share with my closest friends." He passed identical masks to each of the gang. "I couldn't have done this without all your help, guys," he said. "Thanks."

They all donned their disguises and grinned at him.

"What do you say we head down to the beach?" Slater suggested. "There's a burger stand calling my name. Want to join us, Dad? Mr. Belding?"

"Can't, Slater," the principal said. "Mrs. Belding has her special meatloaf in the oven and is waiting for me."

"No, thanks, A. C.," the major declined with a grin. "Maybe next time. After all, it looks like we'll all be in Palisades for a good long time now."

Slater smiled at his friends. "Yeah, Dad. A very good, very long time."